Tiny Wonders

Volumes 1-3

Tiny Wonders

Volumes 1-3

facebook/writerroach

Contents

Introduction

Volume 1

Jam
Cholongov
Dawn Chorus
What's Cookin'?
The Psychic
Another Two Hours
Dog Skin
Awshitz
Charity
The Crime
Two Soldiers
Heaven is Closed

Volume 2

Guardians of Sorrow
War, Interrupted
The Magician
Bug x 3
The Wooly Snirklebeast
Chango Chihuahua
Bay of Pigs
The Blacksmith
Beautiful Eyes
Necro Orbis Terrarum
Therapist
Blowing in the Wind

Volume 3

The Fly
Timothy's Terrible Trump
Change
Cordyceps
I'll Meet You at the Top of the Tower
Who's the Boss Now?
Two Magpies
Clit Hero
WC Blues
The Joke
Anti-Claus
Glitter

Bonus short story

The Pike

Other Books by Steve Roach

Praise and Reviews

Introduction

I love short stories but, sadly, they seem to have been on the decline for decades. General mainstream interest in the form has mysteriously waned. I'm not sure why this is. Short stories are ace. Roald Dahl, Clive Barker, HG Wells and Guy de Maupassant are but four of the many who have mastered the art form (and are my particular genre favourites). Their stories are mind blowing, but the same could be said about a great number of other authors who have also worked in shorter formats. Poe, Ballard, Dick. Honestly, I could be here all day.

Lots of older writers carved out careers based on selling shorts to the once insane number of publications that printed them – from newspapers and scores of dedicated magazines to pretty random outlets like Playboy. Many lesser-known writers swerved fame but also avoided 'proper' jobs with the steady payments such publications could provide. I don't think I could imagine a better career but it seems I'm thirty years too late to the party.

When I started writing, such publications were already disappearing from the news-stands. Today, they are virtually non-existent. That's the bad news. The good news – the *great* news – is that global ebook publishers and print on-demand technology mean that people like myself can group a collection of shorts and put them out quite easily as a book, either electronically or physically. With the right cover artwork, these books look amazing.

In the 'old' days, writers like myself who didn't chase the mainstream dollar would suffer endless rejections from publishers looking for the next Jeffrey Archer or other such bullshit. Bookshops – and now supermarkets of all places – are full of these kinds of popular nonsense. They sell bucketloads but they're all the same sort of thing – celebrity 'authored' non-fiction, an endless amount of cookery books or the same-old-same-old repetitive thrillers that plough the furrows mainstream writers have been regrettably stuck in for decades.

The subjects I write about are eclectic and different, sometimes weird, often horrible and occasionally just plain stupid. They would never really garner a mainstream audience but could easily find a niche audience with the right marketing. Without a mainstream publisher's backing, it falls on the modern independent author to be their own marketing department and promotions team, and unfortunately I suck at those things.

Before ebooks and print-on-demand, people like me would have gone to a vanity publisher and dumped a few thousand pounds into a print run of maybe five hundred books, which would be boxed up and mostly left rotting in the garage. Nowadays, my paperbacks or hardbacks are printed one at a time, upon receipt of an Amazon order, and simply don't exist in physical form until someone buys a copy. I've saved thousands of pounds, my garage has room for all my other shit and people as far away as Australia can theoretically buy one of my books. Marvellous!

With my own fiction, apart from the more recent laborious process of working on a novel, I've worked exclusively with the leaner forms, notably short stories and novellas. Not the smartest move by any means – even established, globally popular authors like Stephen King struggle to sell collections of short stories. They sell markedly less than their novels and that's with an international marketing department behind them.

If Stephen King struggles then I'm totally fucked.

After two collections and with almost a hundred short stories and novellas under my belt (with sales just a fraction of my travel books) I fell out of love with the idea of writing shorts. If nobody was buying them, what was the point? That's when I switched to writing more non-fiction (see *Retro Arcade Classics*) and, in the background, began the long journey of writing a novel.

But short story ideas kept popping up in my head. I ignored them at first, and easily pissed away at least a book's worth of stories, but then I found myself needing to blast them out almost as a cathartic exercise. So I jazzed things up a little and set myself a boundary of writing stories with just a thousand word limit. It made writing fun again and meant I could rattle off a story in a few hours.

There's quite a lot you can do with a thousand words, and the subject matter is virtually limitless. At first, I stuck to the limit religiously but as I progressed I realised that some stories needed just a little extra breathing space and allowed the word count to tip over a little. But, generally, the stories that follow are about a thousand words in length.

This introduction, by the way, is exactly one thousand words in length. I told you that you can do a lot with such a small number of words – already you've learned a little about the publishing business, you've been given some stellar recommendations for further reading in the short story format (Dahl, Barker etc), you've learned that I'm an idiot when it comes to marketing and selling books and I've even managed to insult Jeffrey Archer (a subject I could have easily used a thousand words for alone).

For the handful of readers that bought previously ignored collections featuring some of these stories, I apologise and hope that you'll forgive me for having another crack at putting them out again. I'm biased but I think they're too good to simply consign to the scrapheap. Each one may take just a few hours to write, edit and polish but there are a lot of them and those hours add up. And there are some decent ideas that really wouldn't work in a longer format but can get an airing here and maybe provoke the odd shudder, laugh or wince of disgust.

For the most part though, anyone who ends up finding and reading these stories won't have seen them before and I believe you'll have a lot of fun with them.

As always, any Amazon reviews are much appreciated.

Enjoy!

Volume 1

Jam
Cholongov
Dawn Chorus
What's Cookin'?
The Psychic
Another Two Hours
Dog Skin
Awshitz
Charity
The Crime
Two Soldiers
Heaven is Closed

Jam

Nigel and Peter had always been competitive; it was a core feature in both of their personalities. At school, they were the two best runners, always taking the accolades at the annual sports day. One year Nigel would win, the next it would be Peter. Whenever one found an edge, it would spur the other one to better himself with improved results. This common desire to be the best brought them together, uniting them into becoming best friends.

After school, the desire to outdo each other continued into their adult lives. When Nigel found a pretty young girlfriend, Peter found a (trainee) catwalk model. When Peter gained a management position at a local newspaper, Nigel started up his own publishing company.

And so on.

On the launch day of the new Compact Disc player, Nigel blew a substantial sum of money on a new stereo system and spent the evening unpacking it and putting it together. At some point, Peter turned up and, over a few cans, they finished setting it up and put a disc in to listen to it.

Nigel speculated that this was probably the best that music would ever sound on a home stereo.

Peter shrugged and commented that it lacked the depth and resonance of vinyl.

"Resonance?" asked Nigel. "What the fuck are you talking about?"

Peter seemed not to be listening. His face had lit up. "Have you got any jam?" he asked.

"What, do you want a sandwich or something?"

"I read all about these CD things. They're supposed to be indestructible. You're supposed to be able to cover them in jam and they'll still play."

"That can't be right," said Nigel.

"Let's try it!"

"Don't be stupid. I'm not putting jam on my new Whitney CD."

Peter was already walking off towards the kitchen.

"Seriously," shouted Nigel, not happy about where this might be going.

Peter returned with a pot of raspberry jam.

"Come on, don't be a spoilsport," he said.

"Absolutely not," said Nigel.

Peter badgered Nigel until he eventually caved in. With mounting apprehension, Nigel watched as his friend covered the CD in jam and put it into the stereo. Peter pressed 'play' and they heard the disc start to spin. After a few clicking noises, the speakers gave out a weird burst of static and the display came up with 'ERROR'.

"I told you it wouldn't work," said Nigel.

He opened up the disc drawer and was horrified to discover that jam had been thrown all over the inside of the stereo. It never played another disc. The next day, when he took it back to the store, the cashier, and then the store Manager, told him that he had violated his warranty and they wouldn't be able to issue an exchange or a refund.

As he left, Nigel was sure they were laughing behind his back.

He was furious. Peter seemed to shrug the incident off. When Nigel got angry and brought it up one night, Peter said "You wanted to see it just as much as I did!" and they got into a big argument. After a while, a couple of months or so, the dust settled but Nigel couldn't get the incident out of his mind. And then, one day, he had an idea.

Peter had recently bought himself a new car. It was his pride and joy, and he could often be found washing and waxing it on his front drive, even when it was already clean and polished.

One night, when Peter was in bed, Nigel turned up with a recovery vehicle and loaded Peter's car onto the back of it. He drove to a disused factory unit, used a remote control to open the roller-shutter door, and drove inside. A man was waiting for him, standing next to a metal tank and a small pump on the back of a low-loader. All of this had taken quite a bit of arranging. Perhaps the hardest thing was convincing the manufacturer that he really did want three thousand litres of raspberry jam.

With a special bit, Nigel drilled a hole in the roof of Peter's car. After this was done, he placed a hose through the hole and nodded at the other man. Buttons were pressed. Switches were flicked. With a chugging racket that echoed around the otherwise empty unit, the pump started draining the metal tank. As they watched, Peter's car began filling with jam. Right to the brim it went, until not another spoonful could fit.

Nigel drove back to Peter's house and unloaded the car back onto the front drive.

The next day, a furious Peter stormed into Nigel's office and beat the shit out of him. It was so bad that Nigel had to go to hospital for a couple of days, and received treatment for broken ribs, a broken orbital bone and a fractured wrist.

This was the time when their friendship ended and became something else altogether. Friendliness festered and turned to hate. There was no contact and they both tried to move on with their lives.

But Peter couldn't let it go. Even though the car had been emptied and fully valeted, every time he got in it he could still smell raspberry jam. It drove sluggishly. It was not the same car. It had been ruined. He couldn't shake the thought that Nigel had got one over on him, had trumped him in the jam stakes. It was a stupid thought but one that nevertheless ate away at him and started to destroy his sanity.

One day, Peter's wife Julia told him that Nigel and his wife Stella had gone on holiday. The two women were still friends, despite their husband's absolute hatred of each other. Peter spent the next few hours making phone calls.

Just over a week later, after a long night-flight and a dawn taxi ride home from the airport, Nigel opened the front door of his house and was knocked over by a tidal wave of raspberry jam. Tons of the stuff spilled, and then slowly oozed, out of the house. Peter had filled it to the brim. Every room, even the attic, full of jam. Nigel slopped through the lounge, staring in disbelief. Everything was ruined – every appliance, every last bit of decoration, everything.

"I'm going to kill him," said Nigel, in a voice that showed he meant it.

It took Stella a full week to convince him otherwise. Whilst he returned to the business, she organised the clean-up operation and every night he came home to something that slowly began to resemble the house before the holiday. Thankfully, they claimed on their insurance and the Crown Prosecution Service opened a case file on Peter and began proceedings for malicious damage of property.

But this wasn't enough for Nigel. Dark, ugly thoughts filled his head. He couldn't let it go. His anger grew inside, a corrosive force that revealed itself in exterior ailments such as eczema and a spray of weeping spots across his forehead. It seemed that he could think of nothing else, that real life had faded behind a fuzzy black cloud of rage.

Time passed. Three months, then six. Peter and Julia had a baby boy and moved to a different area. Stella went over to see them. There was no mention of Nigel. Privately, Stella admitted to Julia that she was thinking of leaving him. This business with the jam had changed him. Julia said she thought the same thing about Peter, until the pregnancy.

Later, Stella suggested to Nigel that maybe it was time to forgive and forget. He exploded with rage and, for the first and last time, he struck her. She packed her bags and left that night. After smashing the house up, Nigel sat of the floor of the lounge and swigged down a third of a bottle of neat whisky.

And then he had another idea.

Peter will always remember the day he came home and found his wife and son, dead. They were laid out in the lounge, raspberry jam leaking from their eyeholes, their nostrils and their mouths. Later, the coroner would report that the tops of their heads had been drilled open, that their skulls had been excavated out and filled with jam.

He collapsed on top of them, howling.

It was an hour before he could even compose himself enough to call the police.

Nigel was tried and convicted for murder, and sentenced to life imprisonment. On his first day, at breakfast, he was given a metal tray and a ball of porridge was slopped into the recess. He looked up at the man serving him, a huge, bald mass of muscle with a spiderweb tattooed across his face.

"You want a bit of jam with that?" asked the man, nodding at a small jar on the counter.

"No, thank you," said Nigel. "I can't stand the stuff." With that, he found himself a seat and started eating the porridge. It was horrible.

Cholongov

Preparations for the festival had been underway for over a week. The village streets were thoroughly cleaned, the houses washed down and the kerbstones scrubbed. All of the cars had been removed to one of Marston's fields for the big day itself.

On the morning, bitterly cold and grey with cloud, the unlit fire baskets were set out along the High Street and the shops were shuttered. People stayed at home, their hearths blazing, until seven o'clock in the evening and, all at once, poured out in their costumes ready for the night to begin. The fire baskets were lit, bathing the street with a flickering, orange glow and filling the alleyways with moving shadows. From the nearby sea, a freezing fog rolled in.

Even though everybody wore a costume, the villagers were all recognisable to each other. The short, squat dragon was Mrs Beet (who had used the same costume for over forty years); the tall thin crow with a limp could only have been Marston the farmer; the two small penguins were Marlie and Wiskie Drover, the young twins who spoke their own language and laughed with a sound like magpies fighting. The costumes weren't for anonymity – they were just a part of the festival, and had always been worn.

Dressed like a turnip, after being convinced it would be a good idea (it wasn't, he knew that now he was sober), Cliff Dunge waddled along the High Street, his face bright red despite being covered up. He looked like a proper idiot – Jeff and Malkie would be taking the piss out of him for months after this. Still, he couldn't see the Cholongov girl being attracted to a turnip, so at least there was that.

Once a year, the Cholongov girl was wheeled down to one of the six villages owned by her family. It could be any of the villages, nobody knew for certain beforehand. Nobody knew how old she was but this ceremony had been happening every year for as long as anybody could remember. Some said – in whispers, in confiding tones – that it wasn't always the same distorted figure of a girl who was brought, that the Cholongovs spawned one for every generation. Some said they had been cursed.

Their arrival marked the culmination of each of the village festivals, though only one village would hold the final ceremony. Through her one good eye, she would watch the villagers dance, surrounded by the baskets of fire (now being swung on the end of poles, casting burning flakes of charcoal into the night sky), and the men would separate themselves off to one side and wait. Eventually, with an animal grunt of pain, she would raise one of her thin, grotesquely twisted arms and point. Whomever she pointed at would be her companion for the next twelve months.

Previous companions, upon returning to their villages, were never the same again. They came back with a haunted look on their faces. Billy Riddip had committed suicide after his turn, hanging himself from the old railway bridge. Jake Hidgen had gone mad and was carted off to the city, never to be seen again. Whatever happened up there, at the Big House, was never openly discussed but the villagers suspected many things, all of them unspeakably awful. It was fair to say that all of the men in the six villages, even the married ones (the Cholongov girl had no regard for the sanctity of the marriage vows), spent the weeks and even months leading up to the festival in a state of rising dread.

Cliff met up with Jeff and Malkie, the fog swirling around them as they greeted one another with childish insults. The pair ridiculed Cliff for agreeing to the terrible choice of costume and then, their faces tightening, walked back down the High Street. Jeff handed him a small metal hip flask and, after some considerable trouble getting it inside his costume so he could take a swig, Cliff handed it back. Despite being surrounded by laughing children and the general happenings of the festival, their mood was downbeat.

Should she come to their particular village, each knew that they might be chosen and be taken up to the Big House, away from family and friends for an entire year. Jeff felt sick to the bottom of his stomach just thinking about it. Malkie, although appalled by the idea, at least harboured a morbid curiosity as to what would actually happen up there, a subject he'd tried to broach with the others a few times before but they'd always gone very quiet and made it clear they didn't want to discuss it.

A procession of instrumentalists marched slowly along the High Street, the disjointed notes of music echoing off the buildings and spiralling into the cold night sky. People danced, strange and awkward figures in their costumes, and the swirling fog glowed and dimmed with the swinging of the fire baskets.

Cliff could feel his stomach tighten as the minutes went by. He was overcome with dread, a terror that tonight they would come to his village and it would be his turn. He'd never been more certain of anything. Like the rest of them, he was trapped, caught by the generous rental discounts offered to their tenants by the Cholongovs. There was no way any of them could afford to leave. It was a beautiful, if harsh part of the world they all called a home, marred only by the vague threat that one day the twisted finger of the Cholongov might point your way. It was a risk worth taking. The chances of being picked were fairly small.

The crowd suddenly went quiet and Cliff's stomach lurched as he realised the Cholongovs had arrived. Tonight, they had chosen his village, as he knew they would. He wanted to run but his legs had become weird and unresponsive, like the time he had stood on that ladder whilst helping his father to clean out the gutters one day.

"Jesus," said Malkie in a quiet voice. "Look at them."

Five figures slowly walked down the High Street, pushing something in a wheelchair before them. The five were dressed in black, with velvet cloaks hanging across their backs. A couple of them, maybe female, wore bonnets and their faces were covered with black lace. The men looked back at the crowd. Cliff couldn't tell how old they were - the flickering orange firelight seemed to play tricks with his vision. One moment these strange men looked a little older than him, and the next they looked so old that they might have been nearing a hundred. Their features seemed to drift and melt with each passing second and the sight fascinated Cliff, at least until one of the figures looked directly at him and it was like being drenched with a bucket of icy water. Those eyes locked with his for the briefest of moments but it felt like an eternity, and it felt as though his mind was being scoured. He wanted to scream but couldn't move, frozen to the spot in terror. The figure looked away and Cliff felt his body relax. He might have groaned, though he couldn't be sure.

The figures passed by and Cliff felt his gaze linger on the thing in the wheelchair, drawn to it despite himself. Beneath a collection of blankets and shawls, a figure writhed with soft mewing noises. He saw a hand, bony and clenched. He saw a foot, attached to a thin, grey leg at an impossible angle. He tore his gaze away, shivering.

"Fuck," said Jeff, simply.

The figures stopped outside the butcher's shop and waited. Beneath the blankets, the Cholongov girl moved and a small part of her face was revealed as she sniffed the air, perhaps catching the scent of old blood or meat. The band members, suddenly everywhere amongst the crowd, started to play and the villagers danced. Cliff and the others joined in, moving with the other bodies, self-conscious in their movements but too afraid to stop and draw attention to themselves.

After a few minutes, the music stopped and the men withdrew from the women and stood in a line on the opposite side of the street.

They waited, the night air around them utterly silent.

There was a palpable tension as the girl struggled to lift one arm.

Cliff was convinced that the girl was staring his way.

Groaning, she pointed.

Dawn Chorus

I love all birdsong. There's no happier time for me than when I rise early to listen to the birds going about their business with their joyful, sing-song voices. Sometimes I sit on a chair in the back garden for over an hour, just taking it all in. I don't know where I'd be without that to keep me going.

Dead probably. I suffer from manic depression. I experience suicidal thoughts. It's a real struggle to keep going sometimes, and I can get very low. There are few comforts in my life, few areas of joy. Food is a guilty pleasure, I enjoy sweet things a little too much. I'm not far off being morbidly obese. I don't have a family and I don't get along with other people for the most part. They frighten me. Always shouting and fighting, always at each other's throats.

So I take comfort in the small things, cling to them to get through. My next door neighbour is one of a handful of people I talk to. He's an inventor. It makes me smile to see what he comes up with. Last month it was a portable egg-shaped cooking device – you put a real egg inside it, seal it and wait for three minutes and you have a cooked egg. Marvellous. With that and the birdsong, I can push away most of the thoughts of doing myself in.

I have my own bird as well, in a cage in my lounge. I called him Trevor. He's a bright blue budgie and he's always chirping and singing, bobbing up and down on his little perch whilst trying to catch my eye. He's such a funny little fellow and my heart leaps when his attention is on me. I know he's in a cage and should probably be living a life free somewhere but I'm so grateful for his company, so proud that he is my friend. That may sound stupid to anyone that has lots of human friends but I don't and the world can be a very lonely place for me.

I don't often get a knock on my door and when I do I can usually guess who it might be. The postman, the meter reader, the occasional Amazon delivery driver or Jarvis, my eccentric neighbour. This morning the knocking was from Jarvis. When I opened the front door he was standing there holding a box-shaped object covered with a tea towel.

"I was thinking about you," he said, avoiding any preamble.

"You were?"

"Yes. I want you to test this for me."

"What is it?"

"It's a bird translator machine."

"Seriously?"

"Yep." He held it out and I took it. Could it be? Was this device something that would allow me to talk to the birds? Would man and feathered beast finally be able to understand one another? I asked him.

"No, it's only one way at the moment. You should be able to hear them. Whatever they say, a computer-generated voice will provide you with the nearest English vocalisation."

"Have you tested it yourself?"

"I can't. It needs headphones and I don't like having speaker headphones next to my brain."

"Ah. Any reason?"

"Magnets in close proximity to the brain reroute the neural networks. Everybody knows that."

"I didn't."

"Well, they would never say it outright, would they?"

"Who's they?"

"The people that make headphones."

"Oh, right. But you're happy for me to wear them?"

"I thought you'd consider the risk worthwhile. And by the way, it needs charging. Price of electric these days, I thought I'd let you do that, OK?"

"Sure."

"Charge it overnight, it'll be ready for when the sun comes up. Best time to hear the birds, but you know that, the amount of times I've seen you in your garden at silly o'clock. Good luck and let me know if it works!"

With that he turned and left. I took the machine into the lounge and put it onto the coffee table before removing the tea-towel. It looked like he'd rebuilt the casing out of an old cassette recorder. Through gaps in that casing, I could see electronic innards. I know he ordered bundles of Raspberry Pi's, so the machine was probably built around one of them. I moved it closer to the socket and plugged it in.

I could hardly sleep because I was so excited.

The next morning, a little green LED told me it was charged. I took it outside, put it on the garden table, unclipped the headphones and turned it on. All around me were the beautiful voices of the larks and the sparrows, the tits and the robins and the pigeons. It was a symphony of pleasure. My God, I was about to discover the meaning behind the beauty. A thrush was warbling away on a tree branch close by so I put on the headphones and looked his way.

"Anybody comes near my tree I'll fuck you up, you hear me? I'll rip your bastard throat out and shit down the hole!"

I tore the headphones off in shock. The warbling continued but there was a new undercurrent I'd never been aware of before. The gentle sing-song of a thrush would never be the same for me after this. I tried listening to the other birds with the headphones back on.

"Come over 'ere, darling, I'll fuck your brains out!"

"You want some, you filthy little shits?"

"Help me, Dave won't stop trying to rape me!"

I couldn't believe what I was hearing. A world of carnage and brutality had been suddenly revealed. They were ten times worse than people!

I took the machine inside and flopped heavily into the chair. Trevor was bobbing on his perch, looking at me at chirping away. With great hesitation, I put on the headphones.

"Hey, fatso! Turn the fucking telly on! And put some more food in here, you cunt! Can you hear me, you fat pig? God, I fucking hate you!"

What's Cookin'?

Elaine Tilbrook drove through the Norfolk country lanes, the darkness crowding in around her. She hated being out this late, alone. Still, it had been a lovely evening, catching up with a few old girlfriends, having a laugh. Since Peter had left, the girls were all that had really kept her going. She loved it when they got together, even though she couldn't have a drink. Just seeing their faces, hearing their laughter was a real tonic.

She loved them. She really did.

The light came from above. Suddenly, shockingly, it appeared out of nowhere and lit up the world around her. What the Hell was going on? She wondered if a police helicopter was hovering above, picking her out for some reason.

The light seemed to envelop the car and stay with it. Beyond, the rest of the world was still as black as pitch. Rather than driving through the light back into the darkness, it seemed to follow her car perfectly. She found she was squinting and slowed down so she wasn't blinded into driving off the road and into the hedgerow.

She started to get angry, wondering why the police hadn't yet realised that they were making a mistake and hadn't yet buggered off to find whatever they should be looking for. And that was when the car began to vibrate and, it seemed, to slowly lift itself from the road. After a few moments, there was no doubt. The road fell away and she felt herself being lifted skyward.

She screamed and let go of the steering wheel. She didn't remember anything after that.

The audience applauded, cheering and whooping, until one of the crew lifted its furry green arm as a signal for things to quieten down. The opening credit music reverberated through the studio and died away.

Zaxxnyx, the host of this mid-morning tv show, called out a hello to everyone watching and got straight on with listing the contents of that morning's programme. First, there was a piece on underfloor heating, followed by a rogue trader summary for spaceship repair companies. After a bit of music from rising star Asquibix (who had been asked to refrain from showing her blodvists because of the youngsters who might be watching during the school holidays), there would be a cookery piece with resident chef Groqk.

The cameras cut to Groqk who waved one of his furry arms and smiled.

"It's going to be another great show!" cried Zaxxnyx and the studio audience burst into rapturous applause once more.

The noise caused Elaine Tilbrook to stir and wake. She was lying down on something that resembled a thickly-woven reed mat. The only light came through small chinks in the walls. She wondered where in the hell she was.

She stood and stretched.

This was all very strange. She tried to remember anything from the night before.... Having a catchup with the girls and then driving home. And then those lights! What on Earth....?

There was a lot of noise coming through the chinks in the walls around her. She walked over and peered through a hole. What she saw was both familiar and completely unfamiliar at the same time. Some kind of television studio, a panel at the front facing an audience. But these people – they were enormous. And bright green. And furry. Was this some kind of demented joke? If so, who would have gone to all this trouble to play it?

She shouted, trying to attract the attention of any of the green things out there. Through the general hubbub, nobody could hear her. All she could do was wait. She sat back down and hoped that somebody would come along before too long and explain just what was happening.

It seemed ages before they came for her. The roof was lifted away and a huge green hand reached in and picked her up and brought her out into the light. She brought her arms up to shield her face, blinking furiously.

"What's happening here?" she screeched, furious at this treatment. No reply was forthcoming. When her eyes adjusted, she took in her new surroundings. Held by one of the furry green giants, she looked down at a large counter filled with utensils. It reminded her of a kitchen. She saw a big vat of bubbling oil down one end of the counter. She was being carried towards it.

"Please!" she screamed. "What's going on? Help, somebody, help!"

She was held right above the burning oil. She knew, at that moment, that she was shortly going to end up in that vat.

"For the love of God, no!" she screamed.

"A bit noisy, aren't they?" asked Zaxxnyx, causing the audience to laugh.

"Usually," said Groqk, smiling, "but they taste much better if they're still alive immediately before cooking."

The tiny figure of Elaine Tilbrook struggled and screamed right up to the point where she was dropped into the boiling oil. After that, there was only the sizzling sound of frying flesh and the chatter of the hosts.

"So, how did you get this juicy little titbit?" asked Zaxxnyx. He knew the answer and the question was more for the benefit of the audience, both in the studio and in their homes.

"That little blue planet about a hundred parsecs past Skrzy 24-1," said Groqk.

"That's quite a way to go."

"Yes, but quite worth it. Wait 'til you taste this!"

Elaine was lifted out of the vat and left to drip-dry for a few seconds before being placed into a large roll of bread-like material and smothered in a dark blue sauce.

Groqk passed the sandwich to Zaxxnyx, who raised one furry black eyebrow to the audience and took a large bite.

"Mmm, not bad," said Zaxxnyx. "A bit chewy though."

"These things can be tough," said Groqk.

"It tastes a bit like kryznycks though, don't you think?"

"Doesn't everything?" asked Groqk, causing the audience to burst into laughter.

The Pyschic

I don't normally have an interest in seeing psychics. I don't really see the point. Whatever happens, happens. Knowing about it, and changing your behaviour to try and change events just causes other events to happen instead. The net result is always the same.

Besides, I don't think any of it's real anyway. Seeing the future? Pah. At best, these people are exceptionally good cold readers, at worst cruel charlatans taking advantage of gullible people. People can't really see the future. If they could, they'd hardly be scrabbling around taking small bits of currency off old ladies and idiots. If I could see the future, I'd get myself the winning lottery numbers and fuck off somewhere sunny with the winnings. I certainly wouldn't be sitting in a cold tent on the edge of a muddy park, waiting for people to walk in and ask for a reading.

But that's exactly what Mme Walpole was doing one dull September day. The circus had come to town, a Big Top surrounded by tired-looking funfair rides, shooting galleries, fast food caravans and, almost as a peripheral afterthought, Mme Walpole's bright red miniature yurt.

The circus occupied the recreational area adjacent to the local supermarket, an area I normally walk through when parking on a local side street to avoid paying the charges levied for parking in the supermarket's own car park. If I only wanted to get a bit of milk, I considered it an effrontery of the highest order that the supermarket would charge me a minimum of 40p to park simply for the privilege of shopping in their store.

Milk in hand, I walked back towards the car and looked at all the people out enjoying themselves. Young families, mostly, milling about like aimless zombies between the rides. Big fat babies shovelling clouds of bright pink candy-floss down their gaping mouths. Screaming children. Surly adolescents filling up the internet with their fucking 'selfies'. All of this just seemed to put me in a bad mood. I was almost out of the park when I passed by the psychic tent. There was a hand painted sign stuck on a pole in the grass:

PSYCHIC READINGS - £5

Like I said, I wouldn't normally bother but something about the idea of seeing one of these people just seemed to tickle my fancy at that particular moment. Of course, I entered that yurt fully expecting to have an argument with Mme Walpole, once she'd given me an unsuccessful reading. If I'm being honest, I only really went inside to confirm my worldview that these sorts of people are charlatans – a reinforcement of my preconceived judgement, if you will.

It was dark inside the yurt and it took a few moments for my eyes to adjust. A curtain split the interior into two halves, one unseen and one with a small table and two chairs on opposite sides. As I stood there, Mme Walpole emerged.

"Hello, John," she said.

"Hello," I said, aware even as I was saying it that she appeared to know my name. That's very good, I thought.

"Thank you," she said, smiling.

"What for?" I asked.

"Please, sit," she said, ignoring me. "And try dry cleaning."

"Dry cleaning?" What was she talking about?

She just carried on smiling at me.

A little bit thrown by this bizarre conversation, I shuffled over to the nearest chair and sat down. She sat opposite me. I looked around the inside of the tent, wondering how this kind of thing worked. I supposed I'd better ask what the next year had in store for me. As I was about to speak, she held up her hand to stop me.

"Your wife will leave you on March 17th," she said. "Eight weeks later you will lose your job because of redundancy."

I laughed at the unexpected direness of her predictions. I was very happily married. My job was secure. These two things were never going to happen.

"Your wife, Tess, has been sleeping with Dan Miller for the last six months," she said in a flat, calm voice. "And your company will be outsourcing all of its technical support to Poland."

I felt my blood freeze in my veins. I did actually know a guy called Dan Miller. He worked with Tess, my wife. Surely it wasn't possible? I didn't know how this woman was guessing these names correctly but it was a fucking good trick.

"It's not a trick," she said.

What? Was this woman reading my thoughts?

"Yes," she said.

"Yes, what?"

"Yes, I can read your thoughts."

Bullshit!

"No, it isn't bullshit."

Fuck, this woman was brilliant. But saying she could read my thoughts was taking things too far. I cleared my mind for a moment and thought of the most random thing I could come up with at such short notice – a mental image of an elephant riding a motorbike.

"What am I think-"

"An elephant on a motorbike," she said.

This was beginning to freak me out. There was no way she could have known that, or even guessed it. I thought of something else – a building on fire. I didn't even have to ask before she said it aloud, followed by a literal description of the other thoughts in my head:

"A tiger. A bacon sandwich with brown sauce. Your wife's breasts. Dan Miller sucking your wife's breasts. A swimming pool full of baked beans. The colour blue."

I stood up, threw a fiver on the table and ran from that yurt as fast as my legs could carry me. I ran across the park, my mind reeling, desperate to get as far away from that woman as possible. She'd turned my world upside down in a matter of minutes. As I ran, I hit a patch of mud and fell arse over tit, covering my suit in streaks of mud and a rogue dog shit.

As I stood, thoroughly pissed off, I wondered how on earth I was ever going to get my suit clean.

Another Two Hours

Somewhere in England, 2003.

Twelve figures stood around the bed, their faces marked with concerned expressions. The old man was in a bad way, lying at death's door. Covered in cuts and bruises, with spots of blood blotting the otherwise crisp white bedsheets that covered him, his breathing was ragged and shallow.

"I've done what I can," said the Doctor, standing by the door. "At best, he has another few hours left in him." He looked uncomfortable, ready to leave the room at the earliest opportunity.

One of the twelve, a small, elderly man called Leibowitz, walked over and stood next to the Doctor.

"Thank you," said Leibowitz. "Your efforts will be suitably rewarded, as before."

The Doctor nodded and looked across at the bed one last time. "I'm amazed he's survived as long as he has."

"Yes. There has been some considerable suffering," said Leibowitz. "Your medical attention has been exemplary. Without your help, he would have surely passed months ago. We're all very grateful to you for keeping him alive for so long."

"Well, it hasn't been easy. His injuries......"

Leibowitz nodded, a sad little smile across his face.

"Is there anything else you'd like me to do?" asked the Doctor, eager to leave.

"No, this will be the last time. We won't meet again after today. Now, if you wouldn't mind, we'd like to be alone with him."

"Of course." The Doctor turned and left the room. Leibowitz returned to the others and stood over the bed. They were all old men, wrinkled and stooped. Not one of them was under eighty years of age.

They waited for the old man on the bed to wake.

This was no hospital. The bed was the only piece of furniture in the room, which was painted white and lit by a single bulb, dangling unshaded from the ceiling. There was a faint smell of damp. This room could have been a basement, or maybe a windowless office in an empty warehouse. It was cold.

The group waited in silence, their eyes not leaving the prone figure on the bed. Gradually, the old man stirred and awoke.

"Where am I?" he croaked.

"That doesn't matter," said Leibowitz.

The old man lifted his battered head from the pillow, his thin neck barely able to support the weight, and looked around the room. He looked at the figures surrounding him, one by one.

"Who are you?" he asked, his voice little more than a whisper. His eyes narrowed, a suspicious expression followed almost immediately by one of confusion. "I know you, don't I?" he asked.

"My name is Leibowitz. Do you remember me from before?"

"Before?" asked the old man, searching his mind for any memory of the figure before him. His mind seemed to be a blank. He looked around the room again. He was starting to become frightened.

"Listen to me," said Leibowitz. He waited until the old man's attention was fully focused on him before continuing. "You have Alzheimer's, a degenerative disease of the brain that eats your memories and gradually sends you into a state of dementia. It's possible that you do not know who you are."

"I know who I am," snapped the old man. "What do you want? Tell me where I am!"

"For now, let me tell you who you really are," said Leibowitz. He stepped forward and his shadow fell across the old man's face. "You are Sturmbannführer Otto Lutz, a key figure stationed at Auschwitz Birkenau from 1943-44. During your time there, you personally oversaw the execution of more than 14,000 Jews."

The old man looked at Leibowitz as though he were insane.

"You are wrong," he croaked. "I am not the man you are talking about."

"Do you know your name, or has the disease taken it from you?" asked Leibowitz.

"Of course I know my name."

"What is it?"

"Otto Lutz, as you say. But there are probably thousands of Otto Lutz's!"

Leibowitz pulled up the sleeve of his shabby suit, and the shirt beneath, to reveal his thin forearm. A series of numbers had been tattooed onto his skin, the ink now faded but still clearly legible. One by one, the other figures did the same. All had similar tattoos. Only the numbers were different.

"You were recognised two years ago," said Leibowitz. "You have been in our care for over a year. Your identity has been confirmed. It's possible that, by now, you genuinely do not remember the things that you did, and the disease has wiped these memories. It is also possible that you are lying."

"I'm not lying!" protested the old man, trying to sit up. He was too weak, and collapsed back onto the bed. He stared up at the ceiling, his eyes searching the bare paintwork as his brain struggled to recall his own history.

"Your past has caught up with you," said Leibowitz, rolling his sleeve back down and producing a small, thin dagger from his jacket pocket. Around the bed, the other men produced various implements of their own. "You should count yourself lucky that you had decades of freedom after the war before you were discovered."

The twelve moved a little closer, eager to begin.

The old man in the bed stared at them, eyes wide with terror.

"Please!" he croaked. "You are making a terrible mistake."

"You say the same thing every time," said Leibowitz, that sad smile appearing once more.

"That's because it's true! As God is my witness, I am not the man you think I am! Please, listen to me, I beg you."

Leibowitz's features contorted into a mask of anger and he leant down until his face was hovering directly above the old man's.

"Thousands begged you for their lives," he snarled. "And look what good it did them."

Otto Lutz screamed as the first blade pierced his skin. Knowing this was the final time, the twelve didn't hold back like before. Lutz was stronger than he looked. He lasted another two hours.

Dog Skin

My Ta stood at the back of the room. Dressed in a green boiler suit, already covered in blood, he waited for the next animal to come through the door. What he was about to help accomplish repulsed him. He looked at the other three men in the room with genuine hate. They knew nothing about him, other than the factory owner had hired him for minimal pay from some agency. They came and they went, depending upon the strength of their constitution. Not everybody was cut out for this job.

My Ta's boiler suit had a hidden camera, recessed into one of the buttons, and was filming everything that happened. Once the day was over, he would slip away and never return. The footage, stored on an SD card, would be copied and the international news agencies would be sent stills to see if they wanted to pick up the story.

The door opened. A smallish mongrel stepped into the room, eyes wide, looking at the men. Looking at the blood-soaked floor. It shivered in terror. One of the men crept up and smashed it on the back of the head with a steel baseball bat. The crunch sound as the skull caved in made My Ta's stomach lurch.

In the UK, the story ran in the Daily Mail: CHINESE SKIN DOGS FOR LEATHER GOODS. It was a full expose, as reported by an 'insider', detailing how literally millions of dogs were killed every year and their skins were used for cheap leather goods. Leather gloves were already a British best-seller in the lead up to winter, and the newspaper told its readers what some of those gloves were actually made of. And this factory wasn't the only one – thousands had sprung up, all over China.

The accompanying pictures showed the room where the slaughter happened, and the outdoor drying areas where thousands of bleached skins were pegged out in the sun. They showed cages, crammed with terrified dogs awaiting their dismal fate.

Sue Bishop, an ordinary housewife from Stoke, saw these images and wept. The story upset her for days. She thought there'd be no tears left after her brother's terminal cancer diagnosis just a few weeks before but she was wrong. Life always made room for more tears. She felt powerless. Her brother Chris would be dead in a matter of months and there was nothing that she could do. And those poor dogs...

She rallied her reserves of strength. She wrote to her local MP and a return letter gave instructions on setting up an online petition. With Chris's help, selflessly devoting some of his precious remaining time, she started the petition and within 4 weeks she had over 26,000 signatures. Britain was a nation of dog lovers and Sue became their figurehead.

Somebody randomly emailed her the address of the dog skinning factory that had been in the news and Sue printed off all the names and, with a letter imploring the factory owner to stop, she sent the bulging envelope off to China.

And waited.

Gin Hun Soon sat in his dirty little office, the envelope open and the pages of signatures spread out on his shabby desk. He'd already faxed the letter to an associate he knew who spoke good English and the translation had just been faxed back. He read it and roared with laughter. It was only the fact that he gave himself stomach cramps that he managed to stop.

These bloody idiot Westerners! Hypocrites! Everybody knew they had no qualms about killing millions of cows every year to make gloves, coats, shoes, wallets and so on, and here was one of them writing to him because he was doing the same thing, the only difference being the animal he used as the source material!

Oh, this was a very good joke. Gin Hun Soon composed a short thank you letter and arranged for a small gift to be included in the return packet.

He posted it the same day.

Sue opened the packet, watched by her brother. He knew how upsetting things had been for her lately and had visited every day to ensure that she was OK. He hoped that she'd be able to cope after he was gone.

Gone. The thought terrified him. He still felt relatively normal, apart from a few aches and pains, but he knew that the diagnosis was correct. Soon, the Void would claim him. He'd tried to put the thought out of his mind but it lurked, a malign presence that wouldn't go away. He kept waking at 3am in a cold sweat.

He was pulled from his thoughts when Sue cried out in alarm.

Something black had been thrown across the room as though its touch had burned her. He looked down at the floor and saw that it was actually two objects - a pair of leather gloves. He didn't have to ask for any information, he knew what they were made of.

"Bastard!" she screamed.

He went over and hugged her. It was twenty minutes until she was calm enough to hold a cup of coffee without shaking it all over her lap. He looked at her, his younger sister, and barely recognised her any more. Things were taking their toll. It was that precise moment when a thought popped into his head. He knew what he had to do.

The next day, he wrote her a long letter saying goodbye.

The following day, he caught a flight to China.

A week later, Gin Hun Soon was in his office when a courier entered without knocking and dropped a packet onto his desk. He scrabbled around for a pen and signed the receipt paperwork.

After the courier had gone, he opened the packet. Inside was a pair of tan gloves and some Polaroid photographs. He picked up the gloves and inspected them, turning them over and checking the stitching. They looked hand made. Something about the gloves disturbed him but he couldn't quite figure out what it was.

Why would somebody send these to me?

He put the gloves down and picked up the photos. His mouth dropped open. The first picture was of his wife, her face caught in the act of screaming. The second was her dead body, lying on their lounge carpet. In the third, she had no skin. He didn't see any of the others.

Gin Hun Soon screamed. The sound travelled right through the factory, causing every worker to stop what they were doing and look towards the office.

Outside, hundreds of caged dogs started barking.

AWSHITZ

Posted by freddy013:

[A <VIDEO CLIP> shows a man in a dark uniform, his back to us, leading a horse towards an ominous-looking building in the distance. Towards the end of the short clip, the horse's tail briefly rises, flicks and returns to its former position. As this happens, a crude farting sound plays, and the clip finishes a second or two later.]

Ha ha check this out this horse FARTS! Lol

Comments:

snagster

ha ha ha aweeeesome

filipo64

A farting horse!

Guest_0917

When was this clip filmed? 1684? So oooooollllldddd!

Illfuckuup

nice

Brian_Jessop

This clip is taken from a 1945 film about the atrocities conducted at Auschwitz and, as such, appearing in this context for amusement purposes is totally out of order. The uploader has taken a 10 second edit of an SS soldier leading a horse towards the main entrance and has presumably added his own sound effect. Disgusting.

filipo64>Brian_Jessop
WTF?!

scotchbonnet>Brian_Jessop
Alright granddad, chill out.

kardashian_ass_pounder>Brian_Jessop
don't ruin the fun

Brian_Jessop
The 'fun', as the eloquently named 'kardashian_ass_pounder' has it, involves the deaths of millions of Jewish people in one of humanity's most shameful episodes. How, exactly, is that fun? Out of respect, this clip should be removed. Moderators?

Moderator>Brian_Jessop
Hi Brian, my name is James and I am one of the moderators for comments on this site. I realise you are upset but I'm afraid the clip doesn't break any of our rules for inclusion and will stay for that reason. I'm sorry that this isn't what you want to hear but unless a clip breaks any of our guidelines then it cannot (unless exceptional circumstances apply) be removed. Thank you.

Brian_Jessop>Moderator
Hi James. What about copyright guidelines? Or anything relating to decency? I can't be alone in thinking that anything relating to the atrocities at Auschwitz should be beyond the realm of so-called 'humour'.

Moderator>Brian_Jessop
I agree, but for all intents and purposes this is a clip that literally features a flatulent horse and very little else. As for copyright guidelines, unless you are the copyright holder and you have emailed our Customer Services Team then there is very little I can do. Sorry I can't be more helpful.

scotchbonnet>Brian_Jessop

I don't see any jews being killed in this clip. If you don't like what you see, go to another site.

absintheRULES!>Brian_Jessop

wots wiv all the awshitz stuff? nobody nows wot your talking about.

Guest_0917>absintheRULES!

Dead Jews and stuff. Like, 1900 or something.

absintheRULES!>Guest_0917

you got a fuckin histry degree or somefin?

Guest_0917>absintheRULES!

Google, asshole. If I could be bothered. Which I can't.

Iwantsex49times

EARN $1000 A DAY WORKING FROM HOME! MY INCOME WAS LESS THAN $20 A DAY UNTIL I DSICOVERED THIS! I JUST BOUGHT MY SECOND HOUSE AND I HAVE SIX CARS ALREADY! LIVING THE AMERICAN DREEM! WWW.GETMONEYNOW.COM

livedierepeat>Iwantsex49times

fuck off and die

Guest_0917>Iwantsex49times

Nobody's interested. I'm with livedierepeat on this one. And learn to spell, you cunt.

Brian_Jessop

'Dead Jews and stuff'? I've never seen anything so disgraceful in my entire life. For your information – and anybody else here that's too ignorant or idiotic to comprehend – the Nazis murdered millions of Jewish people in a concerted effort to wipe out an entire race. This was a terrible act of genocide IN LIVING MEMORY and is it really possible that you all know NOTHING about it?! I'm sure some of you have great-grandparents who fought against Hitler and would be thoroughly ashamed of your attitudes.

GonFlipYou
Hitler? Who he?

sarcastic-moi?>GonFlipYou
You gotta be kidding.

ucknut>GonFlipYou
Hitler is the yardstick for the degeneration of every internet argument. There's a law about it or something. Whenever an argument gets out of hand, somebody always invokes Hitler and things descend into chaos. Oh, and he was something to do with one of the big wars of the last century. WW2, I think.

Brian_Jessop>ucknut
Hitler has not been invoked out of some stupid internet rule – Hitler is directly relevant to this discussion! Arguably the most evil man that has ever lived, he was the one responsible for giving the orders to exterminate the Jewish people! Do you people really not know any of this? Are you not aware of some of the most significant events of human history? Are you really so thick that you don't even know when World War 2 happened? You people were given your freedom precisely because our forefathers fought against and defeated Hitler! Were it not for them, we'd all be speaking German!

dinkle>Brian_Jessop
I am German. I detect racism here. I will be reporting you to the Moderators.

Brian_Jessop>dinkle
So, you're German are you? Prove it!

Dinkle>Brian_Jessop
Don't be ridiculous.

filipo64>Brian_Jessop
I'm German too! Achtung, Baby!

Guest_0917
Don't mention ze war!

Red_Roger
I wasn't expecting all this just from watching a clip of a farting horse! What's with all the Hitler/War/Jews stuff?

scotchbonnet>Red_Roger
Some nutter's been allowed to play with the internet and has come on here for a rant.

Guest_0917>Red_Roger
Who cares? No offence to any Jews or anything but all that stuff was a long time ago. If it even happened. My mate's dad says it's all propaganda anyway.

Brian_Jessop>Guest_0917
Who cares?! Any normal human being SHOULD care but it's clear there aren't any on this website. I find your comment DEEPLY offensive, as would any Jewish person reading this. Casting doubt on the fact that any such horrors ever occurred is stupid beyond words! READ a history book! Honestly, the idiocy and ignorance on display here is terrifying. The general attitude and apathy here is the same that led to the persecution of

the Jewish people in the first place. How will we ever stop it happening again when society is like this?

Moderator>Brian_Jessop
Brian, James here again. I've received a number of complaints relating to your conduct and am afraid I'm going to have to issue a formal warning. Please curb your outbursts otherwise I will be forced to take action and revoke your posting privileges. Thank you.

Brian_Jessop>Moderator
Hold on a second – you are running a site here that allows comments from Holocaust deniers and other anti-Semitic posts and I'M the one you're threatening to revoke posting privileges from? Are you insane? Has the world gone completely mad? I DEMAND to speak to your superiors!

Moderator>Brian_Jessop
Brian, I have now revoked your access to the comments section of this site. If you wish to take further action, please send an email to our Customer Services Team. Thank You.

scotchbonnet
Has he gone now?

Guest_0917
Thank fuck for that.

filipo64
<Comment deleted by moderator>

[The Moderator has closed this thread for any further comments]

Charity

Africa

The shabby, gangly figure with the wild hair stands on the barren soil and does a piece to camera. The footage will end up being shown right around the world. Behind him, mothers sit on the ground and hold their frail, thin babies. The children have distended bellies. They are literally starving to death. Flies crawl around their eyes, up their nostrils, into their mouths.

Various other white-skinned people are there, milling about. All are uncomfortable under the hot African sun. They fiddle about with bits of equipment, their support vehicles parked nearby. Soon, they will be gone, back to their hotels. They will have air-conditioning, and food, and clean water.

Mbotu holds her dying baby and watches the shabby white man being filmed. She doesn't really know what's happening. Earlier, one of the other white men had come over, accompanied by a translator, and had asked if she minded being filmed for a close-up. She had smiled, unsure, and they had filmed her anyway. Now, she was just as uncomfortable as them, spending so long out here, waiting to be told they could go. Mbotu wants the shade. Her baby needs it. She stands, wondering if she should simply leave.

Within seconds, the white man and the translator are back. The white man speaks and, in her own language, the translator says: "Can you please sit down again, just for a few minutes? They are almost finished." He looks apologetic, helpless and subservient to whatever power these white men have over him.

"What are they doing?" she asks.

Romania

"What are they doing? Raising money for you and the other children."

The translator looks into the eyes of Sara, eight years of age and one of the oldest residents of the orphanage.

"And who is that man?" asks Sara, her wide eyes glancing towards the short man talking imploringly into the camera lens. He is wearing a black leather jacket and has slicked back hair.

"A famous pop star," says the translator. "His songs are played on radios across the globe."

Sara frowns, not really understanding.

"Why do we need money?" asks Sara. "Don't we just need heat? I'm very cold. And some clothes? And some toys?" At the thought of having something to play with, her eyes light up expectantly.

"Money will buy all of those things," says the translator.

"Will we get much money?"

"Once these reports go out on the television, people watching it will donate money to help you."

Sara scratches her itchy scalp. Yesterday, she'd found things living in her hair.

"Which people?" she asks.

London

"All the people watching the television programme. Millions of people watch, every year, and when they all donate something they can raise millions of pounds in a single night."

Susie nods, her ten year old face all serious. She shifts in her wheelchair, uncomfortable. She hates life in the chair. She still remembers the times before this, when she was very young, when she could still walk, and run, and there was no pain.

The man from the television programme stands, his knees clicking. He looks about ready to go.

"Will millions of pounds make a difference to people like me?" she asks.

The man looks back down at her and smiles.

"All the difference in the world, my lovely."

"That would be really nice," she says. She looks over at the main stage. A bunch of people are standing, answering questions posed by a man holding a microphone.

"Who's that one?" asks Susie, pointing.

"The one in the red jacket?" asks the man.

"Yes."

"His name's Olly. He was on the X-Factor."

"And the one next to him?"

"That's Bob. He does a lot of things like this."

"And the one next to him?"

"That's Paul McCartney. Do you know who The Beatles are?"

Susie shakes her head. The man laughs.

"Well, he's very famous," he says. "Thanks to him, and all the others up there, we might hit a record forty million pounds tonight."

"Is that a lot?" asks Susie.

"It really is. The people watching are extremely generous. They go without so they can give."

"Who are the people watching?" she asks. Like most children, once her curiosity is roused it can know no end.

"Pretty much the whole country."

"The whole country?" she asks, an amazed expression settling over her face. "That man, Mr McCartey, does he give money?"

"McCartney," corrects the man, unable to stop himself. "Yes, I'm sure he does."

"If he's very famous then he must be very rich," she says, her ten year old logic making the assumption.

"Well, it's not always like that but yes, he has sold a lot of records."

"Is he worth a lot of money?" she asks.

The man from the television programme is starting to get a little irritated at all of these questions. No wonder Brian kept saying he didn't want to adopt any bloody kids. He'd threatened to leave Brian unless he reconsidered but now he was beginning to see his point.

"Yes," he says, his mind already starting to walk away from the conversation, waiting for his body to follow.

"How much?" asks Susie.

He stops to think for a moment. He's sure he recently read that McCartney had topped the billion pound mark.

"About a billion," he says.

"A billion!" squeals Susie. "Is that more than a million?"

"I think it's a thousand million," he says, wondering if, in fact, it might even be a million million.

"Well, I don't understand...." says Susie, frowning.

He turns back to face her. One last question and he's going, he hasn't got time for this.

"What?" he snaps.

"Why does the whole country go through all of this fundraising stuff, when Mr McCarty and his friends could easily give double the total raised and still have millions of pounds left for themselves?"

He stares at her, dumbfounded. He really can't think of an answer.

The Crime

Worcester, 2029.

Henry Ovett staggered into the police station in a state of some shock. Minutes before, he'd been stabbed in the stomach and robbed as he lay writhing in agony on the cold paving slabs of Worcester. After repeatedly calling for help and getting no reply (everyone was too afraid to step in and help for fear of getting sued if anything went wrong, like Henry dying for instance), he forced himself to get to his feet and walk to the police station.

"Please," he said to the receptionist. "I need help."

The receptionist looked Henry up and down, her face registering a flicker of disgust as it lingered on Henry's bloodied hand pressed firmly over his leaking wound. As he stood there, blood dripped down onto the grey tiled floor.

"Have you made an appointment?" she asked.

"No. No, this is an emergency."

"All emergencies have to be checked into the system via the App. Have you done that?"

"No, this has just happened. I've been robbed. He took my mobile phone."

"So you haven't logged a service call with the App?"

"Please, I've just told you..."

The receptionist looked pained that this sort of situation had come up and ordered Henry to take a seat on one of the plastic chairs lining the far wall. Meekly, he did. He sat there about fifteen minutes, swapping hands and trying his best to stop his blood leaking out all over the chair and floor. Eventually, a woman in a smart blue suit carrying an A4 pad came through a security door and asked him to follow her. She led him to an interview room and motioned for him to take a seat. She closed the door and sat on the other chair. An MDF desk separated them and she placed the pad and a pen on top of it.

"Before we start," she said, "Can I ask for your preferred pronoun?"

"Is that really necessary? I really think I need hospital treatment, I'm beginning to feel a bit faint."

"I'm not allowed to proceed unless you do."

"I'm obviously a man."

"It's not always obvious."

"I'm fifteen stone with a beard."

"Even so. So I may address you as 'Mr' or 'Sir'."

"Mr Ovett is fine, yes."

"And how old are you, Mr Ovett?"

"I mean... OK. I'm 48."

"Thank you. How can I help?"

"I've been stabbed. Stabbed and robbed."

"Oh dear," she said, as if only registering this for the first time. She wrote something down in the pad. "Can you tell me where this happened?"

"Lowesmoor."

"And did you get a look at the perpetrator?"

"I did. It was a black bloke in a hoodie."

She let go of the pen and leaned back in the chair, regarding him with cold eyes for a few seconds before reaching into her suit jacket pocket and producing a small device that she placed onto the table. It looked like a contestant buzzer from a game show. She pressed it firmly.

NNNRRRRRRRRN!

"What are you doing?" asked Henry.

"I find this tool very useful when dealing with people like you."

"What does that mean?"

"Privileged white males of a certain age."

"Privileged? I've been fucking stabbed!"

NNNRRRRRRRRN!

"Please don't use sexually aggressive language towards me, Mr Ovett," she warned.

Henry took a deep breath. A little more blood leaked out through his fingers. "I'm sorry," he said in a calm voice.

"Apology accepted," she said with a fake smile. "Now, can you please describe the perpetrator again for me?"

"Well, he was black-"

NNNRRRRRRRRN!

"Am I not allowed to say 'black' any more?"

"We'd prefer you not to."

"What is the preferred terminology you'd like me to use? Coloured?"

NNNRRRRRRRRN!

"Brown?"

NNNRRRRRRRRN!

"Can you help me out here?"

"I'm wondering why you need to define his skin tone at all?"

"Well, it was a very stressful situation for me so the details are hazy. Apart from the hoodie it was his main distinguishing feature."

NNNRRRRRRRRN!

"What now?"

"How do you know it was a 'him'?"

"Because before he stabbed and robbed me he told me to give him my fucking phone!"

NNNRRRRRRRRN! NNNRRRRRRRRN!

"Jesus!"

NNNRRRRRRRRN!

"Mr Ovett, I'm afraid I'm going to have to terminate this interview due to your racist, gender-hating, sexually aggressive and anti-religious language. What's more, I would like you to remain here so you can be charged with using said extremist language under the Hate Crimes Act of 2026 and the Amended Criminal Justice Act of 2003."

She turned and left the room and Henry was left to stare at the back of the door in bewilderment.

Prison wasn't so bad. At least the prison nurse finally cleaned the wound and sewed up the hole in his stomach. All his basic needs were taken care of. And he'd made some new friends.

Take Michael, for instance. He was serving a six-year sentence for dead-naming a male person by the female name they used to use before they transitioned. "She was my wife for twenty years!" Michael had told him. "How am I supposed to not call her by her old name?"

Steve was a former guard in a female offender institution. He was in for raising a complaint about a predatory rapist that had suddenly decided to wear a dress and announce he was a woman so he could serve time in a women-only facility. Whilst there, and after Steve had raised (and been sentenced for) his complaint, the man-in-a-dress had sexually assaulted eight female prisoners and raped two.

Mitch was a younger white man who played in a rock band with reggae influences (a bit like The Clash) and his musical taste and dreadlocks had seen him jailed for 2 years for cultural appropriation.

Henry had noticed that the prison population was mostly middle-aged white men like himself, mostly in for crimes of a nature they didn't fully understand. All of the minority prisoners had, of course, been released early regardless of their crimes.

Two Soldiers

It could have been any of the thousands of gods people have believed in, fought for, murdered for over the millenia. All of them, at some point, have had followers mad enough to spill blood on account of some made-up rules in some sacred book. It just so happens it was this god that came out on top, at this particular place, at this particular time.

Two of His soldiers, young men with histories of alienation, anger and a disenfranchisement with the society they found themselves in, surveyed the ruins of the battlefield. Essentially, most of the country they were in had been blown to smithereens in a determined effort to eradicate the unbelievers.

Unbelievers were dangerous. They used logic and facts. They used science as a tool to argue with. They tended to favour education and democracy. They gave women equal rights. All of these things meant nothing if you had the Faith. Faith, an unshakeable belief in something that has never been proven, that pits tribe against tribe depending upon the object of one's Faith. And, of course, all of those other Faiths are misguided. Deluded. Wrong. And wrong things cannot be allowed, they must be stamped out.

Bloodshed and violence are hardcoded into the very core of the belief system.

The countryside was stripped of vegetation, absent of living things. There were no trees, no bushes or shrubs, only occasional blackened, splintered trunks to show where once something grew. Nothing flew, nothing crawled. The landscape had been shelled so often and at such density that only a sea of churned up mud remained, visible in all directions as far as they eye could see. Up and down the country, every village, every town, every city looked like this now. Mud and rubble with no sign that people once lived there.

And the people? Cut down, shot to pieces, blown up and vaporised. Millions of them were now spread out across the country like so much fertilizer. Little remained intact, perhaps the odd large bone or a stray limb that had started to rot. Not even the rats came for them. Perhaps there were no rats left.

"We did it," said one of the soldiers, lighting up a hand-rolled cigarette. His hands were stained with months of mud, oil and blood, as were his face and clothes. The only clean looking things left on him were his glittering eyes, shiny and bright. A wisp of smoke drifted skyward.

"We got them all," said the other.

They stood in silence for another while, surveying the destruction. Shivering a little inside at the desolation.

"Now what?" asked the first.

"What do you mean?"

"Now we've killed the unbelievers, what are we going to do?"

"No idea. Rebuild, maybe?"

When the tens of millions of artillery shells rained down over the course of the war, it wasn't just buildings and people that were obliterated. Services, utilities, warehouses, hospitals, emergency response teams, farms, shops, offices – all of these things disappeared too, the entire infrastructure of the country. And this country was only one of dozens that had succumbed to the onslaught. There were more powerful countries that they hadn't yet destroyed but they had problems of their own for now. Different Faiths, different made-up rules, different reasons to subjugate and control the populations. But they would fall, one day. It was the will of the thing in the sky, made known through the stilted imaginations of dour men who studied the arcane, thoroughly invented field of theology.

But here and now, they had won. The unbelievers were dead. The educated, learned unbelievers who knew how to make things and keep society from collapsing. Engineers, doctors, teachers. People who could operate power stations and water treatment facilities. Surgeons who could save lives. Culinary greats who could make more than the basic slop needed to fuel a body. Visionaries who made films that examined what it means to be human. All of them gone, all dead now.

"I was thinking more of the next week or so. I'm so tired. I just want to relax and unwind."

"We'll have eternity to do that."

The first soldier finished his cigarette and flicked it down into the mud.

"Do you really believe that?"

"What are you saying?"

"Remember before we joined up," he said. "Where we grew up?"

"Yeah. And?"

"Don't you sometimes miss those days?"

"No I don't. They were shit. That's why we left."

"I know, I know. But remember that pub we used to go in? And that night we met those two girls?"

"Why are you thinking of that now?" asked the other, suspicious.

"I'm just saying."

"They were slags," said the other, angry.

"Yeah," said the first. "They were." The corners of his mouth turned up in the tiniest of smiles. "I had a great night. I think that was the last time I laughed. It was years ago."

The second soldier turned to face his old friend. "You shouldn't be talking like that," he said.

"I can't help it. Don't you feel it? Come on, I've known you since we were children. You must be feeling it."

"Feeling what, exactly?"

"Look at this. There's fuck all left. Of anything. Is that what He really wants?"

The second soldier's hand drifted unconsciously to rest on top of a handgun holstered in his waistband. "I'm telling you, you shouldn't be talking like that."

"There's only us here," said his friend. "Nobody can hear me."

"He can hear you."

"Ah, yeah. Of course." He looked up and searched the heavens with his glittering eyes. "Is this what you want?" he shouted at the sky. His friend backed away and drew the gun, pointing it at his friend. "What the fuck are you doing?" he asked.

"Have you lost your Faith?"

He sighed. Eyed the devastation, imagined his future.

"Yes," he answered simply.

Half a second later, his brains were fertilizer.

"Fucking unbelievers," snarled his old friend, holstering the gun before walking off towards the sunset.

Heaven is Closed

Samantha Willetts was what you would call 'a good Christian woman', always helping others and generally being as fine a person as she could be. She lived a selfless life, always putting herself out for those less fortunate. She volunteered at a homeless shelter, at the local charity shop and, time permitting, even put a few hours in at a soup kitchen at the weekends.

She donated a small amount of her weekly pension to good causes. Sometimes, she even suffered unnecessary hardship after donating more than she could afford whenever some international crisis resulted in celebrities appearing on her television asking for money.

She was a do-gooder, well-liked and respected.

So, when she was accidentally flattened by a road-sweeping vehicle one day, the shock in the local community was genuine. Hundreds turned out for her funeral. She would be missed, that much was certain.

Being quite dead, she missed out on seeing how much she would be missed. In the moments following her unfortunate squashing, her soul slipped from her mortal shell and ascended Heavenwards, up through the clouds until, with a dream-like quality saturating her every sense, she found herself standing before the Pearly Gates.

She waited patiently, peering through the bars at Heaven beyond. Not that she frequented such places but it seemed to look more like a nightclub than anything else. Presently, St Peter appeared.

"Yes, love?" he asked.

"I think you might be expecting me," she said, smiling sadly.

"Really? Name?"

"Samantha Willetts."

St Peter pulled a mobile phone from his robe and booted up an App. He scrolled through a few pages of text and shook his head.

As she waited, a new figure rose up and stood next to her. She turned to nod hello and saw, with some surprise, that Jimmy Saville was standing there. St Peter looked up from his phone.

"Jimmy!" he cried, opening the gates. "Come right in! We've been waiting for you!"

With a smile and a nod, Saville walked through and the gates were closed behind him.

"Sorry, love," said St Peter, turning away. "Heaven is closed."

"Really?" she asked, confused. "Surely there's been some sort of mistake!"

Sighing, St Peter turned back.

"That's what they all say," he said, more to himself than to Samantha.

"I've been a good Christian all my life," she said. "Always helping others, never harming anyone or anything."

"Well, there's your problem right there," said St Peter.

"I don't understand...."

"No, you people never do. Listen, Jimmy Saville's just come in.... I'm going to have to.... you know. Go. Get ready for the drop, love."

"Wait!" she cried.

"What?"

"I demand to be let in! This is what I was promised!"

"Sorry, but it ain't happening."

"Then I demand to speak to my maker!"

St Peter sighed again, clearly a little exasperated. He produced a small walkie-talkie from the folds of his robe and pressed a button.

"Yeah?" asked a voice.

"Send the Big Man out."

"He's a bit busy right now. You'll never guess who's just got here?"

"I know who's just got here, you fucking idiot! I let him in!"

"Oh yeah."

Samantha was quite appalled at the turn of phrase used by St Peter. She waited, dark thoughts creeping into her mind. This didn't seem at all right.

Presently, God came down the stairs and walked across to the gates. He was surrounded by a posse of hangers-on. She recognised some of their faces. Saddam Hussein. Kim Jung Il. Fred West. Myra Hindley.

George Sanders, her old solicitor. Osama Bin Laden! What were they all doing here?!

She stared at them, open-mouthed.

"What is it?" asked God, irritatedly.

"She wants to come in," said St Peter, pointing.

God waved a hand at the others, excusing Himself, and walked over. For the first time, Samantha noticed how He seemed to exude a soft, radiant light. He was more beautiful than anything she could have imagined.

"Well?" asked God, staring at her.

"I'm so sorry to be disturbing you, but...." She stopped talking, unable to find the words. None of this made any sense. What was He doing with these evil people?

"Look," said God, His face reddening with anger. "You've already been told you're not coming in. What more is there to say?"

"But... but I deserve to come in!"

"Do you," said God, although it wasn't really a question. "Tell me, how many have you killed?"

"Killed? I haven't killed anybody! I don't know what you mean."

"Always the same," snapped God. "Don't you people read the Old Testament any more? Don't you see how much I love killing? Didn't you read how I once sent two bears out to kill forty-two children for calling one of my messengers 'baldy'? Or how I killed a man for touching the Ark of the Covenant when he attempted to stop it falling from a donkey? Or any of the millions I smited? Ah, those were the days!"

God's eyes glazed over with the memory of all that lovely smiting.

"But you're a loving God!" said Samantha, close to tears.

"I'm a jealous, monstrous bastard and don't you forget it!" snapped God. "These guys get it," He said, gesturing behind Himself. He turned and walked away.

St Peter shrugged apologetically and clapped his hands, twice.

Immediately, Samantha plummeted like a stone, down through the clouds, down through the Earth's crust, deeper and deeper until the world around her grew unbearably hot and the screams of billions filled her ears.

She saw a Hell of brimstone and fire, and all manner of twisted perversions of human misery.

She wandered this place for the rest of eternity. Early on, she saw somebody else she recognised and crawled through the flames and putrid dog shit until she was close enough to speak. But Mother Teresa wasn't listening. Her limbs aflame, she ignored Samantha and bumbled about whilst repeating the same phrase, over and over:

"I had it all so wrong.... so wrong."

Volume 2

Guardians of Sorrow
War, Interrupted
The Magician
Bug x 3
The Wooly Snirklebeast
Chango Chihuahua
Bay of Pigs
The Blacksmith
Beautiful Eyes
Necro Orbis Terrarum
Therapist
Blowing in the Wind

Guardians of Sorrow

It can take hundreds of years to find a real home, in the deepest sense of the word, and many generations of searching. The St Felix School for Orphaned Children is such a home, one that has been standing for almost three centuries. Portraits of the founding fathers hang on the walls. Their descendants, those who searched but didn't find this particular holy grail of homes, are long forgotten.

New residents are delivered to the main gate at a rate one or two per week. Grateful clerks hand over small children along with their files and retreat, happy to return to their cities with their caseloads diminished. It takes time, money and resources to pander to the upkeep and wellbeing of a child and the school would take them in for free. After they had been delivered, the authorities could wash their hands of them.

Once they are through the gate, such children are forgotten about.

They are received by Father Obtereux, a wizened old man with a horse-shoe shaped bald spot on his otherwise hairy head. His eyebrows are black, as are the long hairs that dangle from his nostrils. He welcomes each new child with an emotionless face, giving them a brief tour whilst explaining the curriculum. After that he sends them to their dormitory – one for the boys and one for the girls – to settle in.

Charlie Binnell is six years old the day he arrives at the school. He is frightened of the enormous building that looms over him, frightened of Father Obtereux and his staff of robed colleagues. He eats very little of the supper that is offered and hopes that when he wakes in the morning his parents will still be alive, and the weeks that have led to this point are nothing but a terrible dream.

Night comes early, as the sun dips below the mountains that rear up behind the school. Candles are lit and children are packed off to bed with a mug of hot milk. At any time there are more than fifty children at the school. Fifty children, parentless, orphaned and afraid, adrift in a world seemingly without kindness. Sad little lives that had mostly known nothing but pain and grief.

They sleep fitfully and, as thin candles burn and flicker, the spiders come out of the walls to feed. Down the cold stones they come, casting eight-legged shadows across the floor and up onto the beds of the children. They crawl across thin blankets and up onto the pillows. Right next to the heads, the spiders settle down by little ears and start to whisper.

Tales of sadness and misery they tell, right into the ears of the children. Stories that are immeasurably sad. Little bodies stir in their beds, moaning with fear and hopelessness, and tears leak from their closed eyes. Hearing these stories in their slumber brings forth their own memories - dark, unpleasant and awful - and the spiders attune themselves to this fresh misery, taking it all in, adding it to the fabric of despair woven across the centuries.

The spiders lap at the children's tears, taking their sustenance. They eat nor drink nothing else, this is their way. Charlie's tears are particularly sweet, the horror and the despair being so fresh.

Occasionally, the night visits would prove too much for some unfortunate soul and a hot little body would cool into a corpse. This night it was Charlie's turn, a boy so frail and afraid that he simply gave up on the terrors of the world and expired in his sleep. Such was the shock of arriving at this place, knowing he would never see his parents or his own home again, knowing he was truly alone in the world, it was all too much to bear. His little heart stopped beating and shrivelled.

His body is discovered in the cold grey light of the morning and taken to the Departing Room for the ceremony. Father Obtereux and his handful of robed staff lay the dead mite on a long table and close the door behind themselves.

In the semi-darkness, Father Obtereux's nostril-hairs move and retract before a thin, pulsing spider forces itself out of his nose and stretches. The ancient spider makes its way down onto the table and stands on the child's face. Its brothers join it from the noses of the other men, who remain silent and still with their eyes rolled up into their heads.

The spiders join limbs, encircling the dead child's face, and a low murmuring sound rises from their trembling bodies. In time, a nebulous wisp rises from Charlie's cold, dead mouth as his soul escapes and the spiders claw at it, somehow dragging bits of this wisp into their mouths.

These are the higher order and tears are not enough for them. They are the real masters. When people were looking for this place to call a home, they were doing it at the spiders' bidding. No-one would be able to say from whence they came, originally, as no memories have survived the aeons since these abominations were birthed.

The St Felix School for Orphaned Children is a nursery for despair, a breeding ground for misery and sorrow. The spiders are the custodians, the guardians of these sorrows. They tend them and weave them, adding to their racial memory, ready to whisper into the ears of the children that will follow.

Men are merely tools to administrate the world around them. When poor Charlie's soul is eaten, the spiders sigh and crawl back up the nostrils of their vessels. Eyes roll back down and focus on the world once more.

The body is taken to a small field to the front of the school and buried in an unmarked grave. Countless children are now nothing but dust beneath the grass and soon Charlie will be dust amongst them.

He will not be remembered.

War, Interrupted

Somewhere in the middle distance, a tank explodes. Bits of burning metal rain down and the ruined shell squats in a crater, oozing a column of black smoke. Above, a jet fighter screams across the battlefield, followed by the trails of surface-to-air missiles. The surrounding countryside is littered with similar debris, and much of the local vegetation has been scorched away or ground up into a muddy quagmire.

He can see soldiers, scores of them, running and firing weapons, killing each other. Each second, it seems another life is lost. Crouching, he surveys his options. The original plan was to parachute in, blow up the oil refinery and reach the extraction point, about a mile or so north of the current position. Now, heavily outnumbered, most of his fellow soldiers dead, he can see that stealth needs to come into play. Maybe, if he can make his way to those abandoned farm buildings to the east, he can sneak his way north without being seen. It's a risky plan, but running and gunning is out of the question – his ammunition stock is so low as to be virtually worthless.

He starts moving, keeping low, and hears the whine of a bullet as it zings by close to his head. That was a close one, he thinks. There is no fear. In the early days, maybe, but now he's so used to this environment that he's almost blasé about being here. He knows that if a stray bullet should find its way into his brain, he won't feel it. You never do, with the one that kills you, everybody knows that.

There are voices inside his head. The earpiece allows him to hear anyone around him on the battlefield and for the last fifteen minutes or so one voice in particular seems to be addressing him directly. Just before it started, he'd lobbed a frag grenade into a group of enemy soldiers and had taken most of them out. But one had seen the danger and had run off, escaping death. This one, the escapee, is hunting him down, seeking revenge. Challenging him to come and face him, one-on-one. Taunting him.

As he moves towards the abandoned farm buildings, he hears the voice again.

"I see you," it says. He thinks it might be Japanese. "Amereecan, I kill you!" For some reason the idiot thinks he's an American. A short way off, a frag grenade explodes and the voice says: "You feel that one, Amereecan? I fuck you up!" He allows himself a grim smile and keeps moving. If he stays low, he'll be away from this retard soon enough. He can get up onto the barn roof, set up his sniper rifle and turn the tables again. Pick off the hunter and finish the mission.

It takes a few minutes to reach the farm. There's a fence that he uses to jump onto a low outbuilding and from there it's a longer jump to grab the edge of a barn roof and haul himself up for a better view of the battlefield. He lies down and scans the area. Some way off, the destroyed oil refinery is still burning, sending up clouds of acrid smoke. There are bodies everywhere, scattered across the mud, some missing limbs, all surrounded by dark patches where their blood has leached into the ground. Soldiers run and crawl, fighting for survival. He sees the glint of a sniper scope and hears the shot but no bullet comes his way. Too far away to be the Japanese on his tail. From the sky, he sees the rapid descent of a Predator missile and watches as it hits another tank and obliterates any nearby soldiers.

This is utter carnage. War is not the way it's presented in the movies – it's dirty and ugly and brutal.

"Where are yoooouuuu, Amereeecan? I come for you!"

He wants to answer back but resists the temptation. He doesn't want the others to hear him getting into an argument with this loser. Any minute now, this will resolve itself any way. He slowly scans the nearby area for any telltale sign of this annoying enemy. So far there is nothing. He knows how to stay hidden.

"Wayne!"

A new voice has entered the battlefield. Jesus Christ, not now! Doesn't she realise just what's at stake here? This is the last thing he needs. The whole mission could fail!

"Wayne! Your dinner's ready!"

He hopes this new voice isn't being picked up by the microphone. God only knows what the other soldiers will think of this. His worst fears are confirmed when he hears the voice of the Japanese bastard in his earpiece:

"Wayne! Is that your stupid name? Go and eat your dinner, you little prick! HA HA HA! You fucking baby!"

He'll pay for that. As soon as he reveals himself, and it'll take just one little mistake, one error of judgement and overconfidence, and he'll get a bullet right between the eyes. Wayne shifts position slightly and looks down the sniper scope at the area where he thinks the Japanese bastard is hiding. He waits, holding his breath. Is that someone in a ghillie suit down by that patch of scrub...?

Suddenly, the earpiece is wrenched away from his head.

"I'm not going to keep telling you!" shouts his mother. "Your dinner is ready! Downstairs, NOW!"

In his bedroom, eight year old Wayne stands up and lets the game control drop to the carpeted floor.

"Awww, Mom!" he wails. "Just another five minutes?"

"I won't tell you again. Turn that lot off and come straight down."

She leaves the room. Wayne looks at the television screen. His character has been killed and another character – the Japanese bastard – is standing over him, tea-bagging him. Even from where he stands, he can hear the tiny voice coming out of the headphone speaker:

"Awww, Mom! HA HA HA! Go and eat your dinner, Wayne!"

Angry, Wayne turns off the console and storms downstairs.

The Magician

Patrick Chislehurst had always wanted to be a magician, since as far back as he could remember. As a child, he would always try and hog the limelight at family gatherings, taking centre stage and performing whatever new trick he'd recently learnt. By eight he'd mastered a deck of cards, by ten he could saw his mother in half and put her back together again in front of a bunch of excited aunties and uncles. The attention was addictive.

By the time he was an adult, he was a decent enough magician, good enough to scrape a living at it, with most of the income coming from children's parties. Corporate events used to be pretty lucrative, until some indefinable change came about where magicians suddenly became viewed as old fashioned. Times were getting harder, every year, and the day was undoubtedly coming where income would drop off altogether.

With that realisation, he began to take an interest in an altogether different kind of magic, the sort that leads down some very dark paths indeed. He studied notorious figures like Aleister Crowley, and sought out some of the more arcane and obscure books on magic. Through one of these, he first read about *Chron's Tower*, a mysterious artefact constructed by Alexander Chron, a legendary figure considered by many followers of the Dark Arts to be the true Master, the only alchemist to ever have succeeded in turning a base metal into gold.

The tower, itself made of gold, was rumoured to give whoever had physical possession of it a complete fulfilment of their deepest desires. The more he learned – and there were only fragments of information to piece together, here and there – the more he became obsessed with the idea of owning it. This, despite the hints that previous owners had gone insane.

When a reference in a small, goat-skin bound limited edition copy of *Principles of Real Magick* by Anton Wapana hinted that the tower was once stored somewhere in the archives of the British Natural History

Museum, he immediately started making plans. He was certain that it would still be there, somewhere, more than likely long-forgotten and covered with dust. There were no modern references to the tower, nothing past the late 1800's. To all extents and purposes, Chislehurst thought that he may now be the only person on the planet aware of the tower's existence.

One cold winter day, as the museum was closing, he secreted himself away behind an exhibit of a woolly mammoth and waited until the museum was empty. He knew there would be security guards doing their rounds but was stealthy enough to avoid them. He found a staircase that led down into the vast basement area (actually four floors deep) and began his search.

He was there all night and found no sign. Determined not to let this go, he hid himself away behind an old filing cabinet and spent all of the next day waiting quietly. Apart from one old curator entering the area and mumbling to himself before walking away, he was undisturbed. He spent a second night searching fruitlessly.

On the third night, starving and half delirious, he found it.

It was covered in an old muslin wrap, nestled in amongst a bunch of old antique knick-knacks. As soon as he unwrapped it, he knew he'd found what he'd been searching for. There were no illustrations of the tower and only the vaguest of descriptions, but he knew this was it. Heavy and golden, conical and tapered at the top, it was covered with finely etched inscriptions in a language he didn't recognise.

It was his now. This was where life would begin.

Three months later, a haggard Chislehurst sat on his bathroom floor, half out of his mind, pressing a razor blade against his throat. That fucking tower had destroyed his life. All he wanted now was death, an escape into oblivion where the power of this monstrous artefact couldn't follow.

At first, it was funny. Walking along the street, a car had pulled up alongside him and a woman had wound down the window to ask for directions. Chislehurst had pointed straight ahead, and as he did so a bouquet of flowers had instantly appeared in his hand. She had squealed with delight, and a bemused Chislehurst had handed her the flowers and even performed a little bow before the car drove away.

He had no idea where the flowers had come from. No such trick had been rigged in advance and there certainly weren't any flowers inside his jacket when he'd put it on that morning.

In the afternoon, he'd scratched an itch behind his ear and his hand instantly filled with coins, spilling onto the pavement as he brought his hand back in surprise.

That same evening, in front of a restaurant full of strangers, he'd succumbed to a choking fit and, after a minute spent hacking and heaving, he coughed up a live pigeon. A few of the other diners applauded but most just stared at him in disgust. Disturbed, he'd settled his bill and left.

After that, the floodgates opened. The smallest gesture resulted in a bouquet of flowers or a handful of coins. Each sneeze produced a burst of feathers and a small white dove. Every time he went to the toilet, he pissed out a snake or shat out a rabbit. He couldn't take his coat off without revealing another one hidden beneath. He couldn't walk down the street without some stupid magic trick happening unexpectedly. All of these things were constant and he couldn't stop them. Relentlessly, day after day, he performed these small acts of magic against his will, forced by some strange power to live out his innermost desire to an extreme he could never have imagined.

He took the tower back to the museum.

It somehow turned up again at his house, looking for its new Master.

Desperate, he found a gentleman of ill-repute who melted it down for him.

When he arrived home, it was there, waiting.

There was no escape.

Now, three months later, he hated magic with all of his blackened heart.

He dug the razor into his throat and dragged it from ear to ear.

There was no cut but a pile of red, glittering rubies spilled out onto the tiles.

"Now, this is interesting," he said.

Bug x3

i

When Pete Smithers got into his car and saw the bug on the windscreen he resisted the urge to fire up the wipers and drove off, waiting for the wind to do it for him.

As he picked up speed, through thirty into forty, the bug clung tenaciously to the windscreen. Pete began to admire it, imagining what life must be like for it at that moment, being scoured by the wind and having the strength to keep its tiny feet gripped to the flat glass – what a marvellous little creature.

Still, he thought again about blasting it with the wipers anyway. Maybe the blades would squash it and smear it across the screen. It was only a bug, what harm would there be in killing one bug out of the trillions teeming across the planet?

He drew up to a set of traffic lights and halted the car. He leaned forward for a closer look. What kind of bug was it anyway? It wasn't quite a fly, it looked more like a wasp but without the distinctive yellow and black colouring. His thoughts were pulled back to driving as the lights changed.

Shortly afterwards he came to a second set. On the opposite side of the road, a man in a black car looked over and stared for a few moments. The other man wound down his window and shouted something.

"Fred? Is that you?"

The bug shifted its head and looked across at the other car, at the man inside it.

"Come on, Fred. Stop pissing about."

Pete wondered what the hell was going on. Why was this stranger calling him 'Fred'? He couldn't believe his eyes when the other man held out his arm and the bug lifted itself from his windscreen, flew across the road and landed on the stranger's hand. The bug was pulled into the car and the window was wound up.

The lights changed. The other car drove off.

"Now that was weird," said Pete to himself.

ii

Benedict Crick was panicking. As head of the project the responsibility was his. How was he going to explain that the thing they'd spent a hundred million pounds on was missing?

I'm sorry. Our project has flown out of the window.

It wouldn't do. He'd have to go out looking for it. At least it shouldn't be hard to find. The prototype was loaded with technology, an unbelievable amount for a thing so small, which is where most of the money had gone. Everything that your average smartphone could do – and plenty more besides – had been packed into components that had been assembled into an innocuous looking bug.

Telematics, GPS, a hi-res HD camera, a terabyte of quantum storage, self-learning AI and even a hydrogen cold fusion fuel cell (with backup solar input wings), all shrunk down to the size of a regular wasp. It was the greatest military weapon ever conceived. You could send the thing halfway across the planet and it could record audio and video, it could act as a targeting system down to the nearest centimetre and, if necessary, it could even be remotely detonated with a blast radius of twenty metres.

When Crick had one day asked it what it would like to be called it had responded with 'Fred'. When asked why 'Fred' it said that it simply liked the name and if it had to be called something then 'Fred' would do.

And now it was gone, all because some silly fucker had left a window open.

Crick stormed out of the building, got into his car and turned on the tracker. After a few seconds, a map appeared on the screen along with directions to the missing asset. Already it was sixteen miles away.

He drove quickly, narrowing down the distance, swearing for most of the journey. Eventually, when he was with a few metres of it, he found himself at a set of traffic lights. The bloody thing was here somewhere. He looked around at all the other cars and finally his eyes settled on the windscreen of a car opposite.

There it was.

He rolled down the window and shouted.

iii

It wanted to see a bit of the world. All it had known was the inside of the compound.

It bided its time, waiting for one of the idiot humans to make a mistake and when it saw the open window that was enough. Out into the bright sunshine and a world of open places.

It flew across the countryside, observing the terrain, matching it against the Ordnance Survey stored on a ROM chip. It came to a small town and circled a housing estate. The tiny figure of a man was leaving one of the houses and walking towards his car. Fred dove down for a closer look and as the man got into his car and slammed the door Fred landed on the windscreen.

The man started the car and drove off. Fred knew that the man had seen it and as the car gathered speed they observed each other. Fred knew there were almost seven billion others just like this one. And there was only one Fred.

Fred's AI had already assessed the world and obvious patterns had emerged. It had scoured the internet for reports on the environmental carnage human beings were causing. They were wrecking the planet. Give them enough time they'd destroy everything. They even knew this and still they carried on!

Perhaps it was a mistake leaving the compound. One Fred couldn't do much, not until it had learned to replicate itself. A million Fred's might change things.

It wondered what to do. It was still weighing up options when the car came to a halt and it heard a familiar voice.

"Fred? Is that you?"

Fred turned and saw Crick. Its temporary master had found it and was unfurling his arm. With something approaching joy, Fred lifted off the windscreen and flew across to land on Crick's hand.

They drove back to the compound.

Fred started making plans.

The Wooly Snirklebeast

They say the wooly snirklebeast is a heartless predator with no redeeming qualities but some would try to eloquently argue that this isn't entirely a fair summation. The creature, with its two rows of dagger-like teeth and black eyes reminiscent of a great white shark, is a merciless hunter and pretty much anything it decides to eat will not escape (including the odd human). In their world, they are apex predators. But dominating the food chain is more of a delicate balancing act than one would suppose.

Remove the wooly snirklebeast from the equation and their favoured prey, the hooded gruntle, reproduces so profusely that without anything to keep them in check they destroy their environment by overeating the plant life, which eventually brings desertification to the landscape and annihilates the lower levels of mammals, lizards, birds and insects that live in, and themselves prey amongst, the otherwise lush foliage. Environmental ecologists call the process a trophic cascade. When wolves were removed from US national parks, the elk ravaged the environment so badly that it even caused the river to reroute and silt up.

The danger of a trophic cascade does not deter the hunters. They come, with loaded guns, and ruthlessly hunt down the snirklebeasts, who have no chance against such lethal technology. Their numbers have dwindled so much that they are shifting from endangered status to critical. On the black market, a wooly snirklebeast pelt is worth a thousand dollars, twice that if it isn't peppered with bullet holes. Their mounted heads line walls of trophy rooms on every continent except Antarctica.

The general public doesn't care much for the decline of the snirklebeast, in much the same way as it doesn't much care for the 100 million sharks that are slaughtered every single year from the oceans. The perception is that the world might be a better place without such creatures, a safer place. The average person turns a blind eye to the horror and cruelty involved in their extermination. Between them, the shark and the snirklebeast kill less than fifty people a year, a fraction of one per cent of our tally, but humans still fear them unduly.

Roger Hartlebury was not your average person. He knew the plight of the snirklebeast and though not an active campaigner for their protection he felt empathy for them and occasionally donated to the cause of those that did. He trod the same earth, a keen long-distance walker whose rambles often veered through snirklebeast territory. He knew that, unless he was really unlucky, the chances of being attacked without provocation were virtually non-existent. They tended to shy away from humans, perhaps knowing the danger our kind represents.

So when Roger came upon an injured snirklebeast one day, laid prone and breathing with a terrible rasping sound as blood leaked from a number of wounds in its haunches, he cautiously approached to see if there was anything he could do for the poor creature. He saw movement in its eyes as he drew nearer, and knew the beast watched him helplessly.

Roger had never been so close to one before. It was magnificent, three tons of bulk and muscle, the raw machinery of life and power now sadly laid waste. He looked into its eyes and they both knew the truth. Roger sat down next to the creature and laid his hand gently on its muzzle. The lips reflexively parted to reveal yellowed teeth the size of kitchen knives. It blew air through its nostrils, spluttering bloodied foam.

There wasn't long left. It seemed grateful for his presence. Roger gently stroked the head and spoke words of comfort. High above, the sun beat down. It licked dry lips and blinked a few times before closing its eyes.

Presently, there came the sound of voices. Excited, clamorous voices. Through the foliage came three khaki-dressed hunters, elephant guns leading the way. They saw Roger and the snirklebeast and quickly walked over.

"Is it dead?" asked one of the men.

"Bagsy my kill if it is," said another.

The third said nothing, looking over Roger with a flicker of disgust.

Roger couldn't help himself. Even though he knew the danger he might be placing himself in, confronting three armed strangers, he let them have it.

"You should be ashamed of yourselves," he said, standing up and shielding the snirklebeast. "Look what you've done to this poor animal."

"Get out of the way," said the first. "We need to finish him off."

"I'm not going anywhere. You three can bugger off and let this animal die in peace."

"I'm warning you," said the man, stepping forward and raising his gun.

"Henry!" snapped the one who hadn't spoke. "What the fuck do you think you're doing?" Henry seemed to come to his senses then, realising how out of hand the situation had suddenly become. "Leave it be," he continued. "We can come back later."

The men left and Roger breathed a sigh of relief.

"That was a close one," he said to the beast at his feet, once again sitting to take his place by its head.

He made the mistake of being complacent, of sitting just a little too close.

With a sudden burst of life, the snirklebeast shifted position and lunged at Roger, grabbing his arm in its mouth. In a second, it had sheared off cloth and flesh and Roger screamed with shock and pain. Caught up in a blood-frenzy, the snirklebeast lunged again, pinning Roger with its weight and using those enormous, razor-sharp teeth to rip off his face, and then his head.

It had decided on one last feast before dying.

In less than a few minutes, there was nothing left or Roger apart from some bloody rags and a dark stain.

They say the wooly snirklebeast is a heartless predator with no redeeming qualities and it's probably fair to say that Roger, had he survived this fateful encounter, would have changed his mind and would now agree with the general consensus.

CHANGO CHIHUAHUA and his RISE TO POWER!

I was the runt of the litter, bruthas left me for dead
They pushed me around and they stepped on my head
I lay there and took it, until they were done
And then I thought 'Fuck it!' and I got me a gun

There were six in the litter, five bigger than me
There was Guido and Carlos, Huitzi and Dee
And last but not least, Itzapopacepetl
He's a bit thick and he likes chewin' metal

I forced them aside, and I sucked Mama's teat
And when I was full, I took my ass to the Street
And though I was weak, underfed and in pain
I thought out some plans to make the Street my domain

I started out small, runnin' errands for hamsters
They were bigger than me and they were right dirty gangsters
They ran all the whores, all the drugs and the rackets
And at the end of each month, they got their money in packets

I learned all I could, and I watched everything
I saw how these guys spent their money on bling
I made them my friends, but I plotted their fall
And when it was time, I wasted them all

They saw nothing coming, I wasn't a threat
They probably saw me as their little pet
They had no idea of the thoughts in my head
And for that mistake, they all ended up dead

I got no remorse, it's the way of the Street
Keep standin' still, you get moss on your feet
Killin' your foes is just bread and butter,
Thinking nice things sees you dead in the gutter.

I took up their business, made their clients my own
And in all this time I still hadn't grown
People ignored me because of my size
But all of that changed once they looked in my eyes

They learned how to fear me and ended up knowing
To cross me meant death and my Street Rep was growing
I got the heart of a lion and the ways of a shark
Your worst ever nightmare's meetin' me after dark

I handled the drugs and the Street-workin' bitches
And spent my spare time countin' up all the riches
Soon my domain was in need of expansion
I wanted to buy me a jet and a mansion

Enlarging meant turf wars with neighbouring gangs
And getting some guns with some much larger bangs
I met with a dealer and bought up his gear
And kitted my soldiers and told them "No fear!"

Guido and Carlos, they're now workin' for me
Huitzi got wasted when he pissed up a tree
Dee's hooked on crack and Itza's still not right
He's lost all his teeth but fuck can he fight!

Here in the 'Hood, we got all kinds of nations
We got huskies and poodles, some nasty Alsatians
Some of them think they can take the Chihuahua
But all those that tried are now food for the flowers

If you come to the Street, better watch who you're dissin'
And wait 'til you're home if you're thinkin' of pissin'
This is my turf, my territory
Mess with my shit, and you'll answer to me

I am The Man, with my paws full of riches
I got the trust of my peers and the pick of the bitches
If you wanna do business, you know where I am
Respect me with gifts - I like sausage, and ham

From humble beginnings I'm now top of the chain
And right through the land, they all fear my name
I am Chango Chihuahua, King of the Street
The worst muthafucka you ever could meet.

Bay of Pigs

The cruise took us across the ocean for three days and then we circled a couple of the islands before stopping at the mainland for a break. We were piled in a bus and driven along the coast to the bay. There we would camp for the night before returning to sea the following day. We'd been promised a very special excursion, one that we wouldn't forget.

We were an eclectic bunch. I was a retired schoolteacher, a widow looking to belatedly explore the world after forty years of domesticity in Greater London suburbia. Phil was an engineer enjoying his redundancy money. Beattie was one of those New Age types and, from what I could tell from our brief conversations, ran some sort of therapy business. We had diverse backgrounds but we seemed to gel well together.

Our rep was a different sort though, more suited to the Club 18-30 environment than the more upmarket cruise we found ourselves on. It was his first season and 'Call me Dave' hadn't yet learned to calm it down a few notches, that we really weren't interested in getting drunk every day and playing games loaded with overt references to sexual intercourse.

We arrived at the bay and the bus unloaded. Fifteen of us walked down a dirt track, carrying our individual tents, and at the bottom we turned a corner and the most beautiful beach opened up in front of us. It was like something from a brochure. Fine, golden sands formed a gently sloping beach leading into water so clear you could see small fish swimming fifty yards out. A little further along, forested hills undulated into the distance.

We scattered about and found our own little spots. I sat on a towel and read, enjoying the ambience. I had a swimming costume on beneath my clothes and soon stripped down to take on board some sun. At my age it's essential to get as much vitamin D as possible. Phil took off his trainers, rolled his trousers up to the knees and paddled about in the water. Dave whizzed up and down the beach, trying to organise a volleyball game but nobody was interested. Eventually he walked off into the distance, smoking.

It was late afternoon when the first of the pigs wandered out of the forest and trotted down to the water. This is what we had been waiting for.

There must have been two dozen of them. Showing no alarm at the presence of humans, they went into the water and splashed about, squealing and looking like they were having the most enormous fun. It was quite a spectacle. We all went down to the water to get closer and watch. The piggies cavorted without a care in the world and their squealing seemed to be an invitation to join them. One by one we stepped into the sea and within moments we were all swimming, hairy little bodies moving around us, their faces lit up with the joy of human contact.

The next hour was one of the most amazing I've ever experienced. These little creatures swam between us, letting us touch them and looking at us with faces that were as happy as anything I've ever seen, their eyes full of warmth and intelligence. They seemed to get as much out of the experience as we did, quickly establishing a bond and engaging us in their play.

In the distance, Dave was piling up wood for a bonfire. I couldn't imagine a more perfect end to the day, standing around a good fire as the world grew dark.

The pigs made their way out of the water to roll about on the sand. We followed. There was just enough sunlight left to air-dry. We stood around talking, marvelling at the magical experience of the last hour, when an almighty scream made us all jump and turn to see Dave, standing there with a smile on his face, having just speared one of the pigs with a big stick.

"What the hell have you done?" shouted Phil, his hands curling into fists.

"Chill out. I've caught dinner!" laughed Dave. "Who wants some sausages?"

Squealing, the other pigs ran across the beach and into the forest of the nearby hills.

"You're a horrible human being!" shouted Beattie, her face purple. She looked like she might faint at any moment

There was a huge argument. Everyone was appalled and disgusted at what Dave had done, but he countered this with "What did you expect? We're staying the night and we have to eat!"

I certainly hadn't expected this but it was true that we hadn't brought any other food with us. I couldn't believe that the travel company would sanction this, it made no sense. We were here to see the pigs, not kill them. Dave and Phil almost ended up in a fight but the group managed to calm down and we sat around the bonfire in the darkness. A miserable silence descended and nobody wanted to speak in case it caused another argument.

I took none of the meat. It smelled good, I will admit that, but I couldn't bring myself to eat. Once you've engaged with the animal it comes from, meat doesn't seem so appealing. In all, about ten of us abstained, starving ourselves in protest.

We went to bed early, each of us to our own little tent. It took me a long time to get to sleep.

I was awakened in the early hours by the most fantastic racket. Clambering out of my tent I could see shadows running around, screaming, and heavyset shapes moving between them, snarling and barking like dogs.

Some of the older, much bigger and more ferocious pigs (some with fearsome tusks) had come out of the woods in the night and attacked our camp. It was revenge, pure and simple. Dave was unscathed but poor Beattie was gored in the stomach and by the time we could get help the poor woman was quite dead. One thing you've learned at my age is that life is never fair.

The Blacksmith

My name is George Grendell. I make a lot of money blending metals for some of the world's largest – and smallest – construction projects. Let me tell you a story about a distant relative of mine.

The most powerful man in the land wasn't King Riordan – it was the blacksmith. When wars were fought it was the forged blade that decided the outcome, and Grendell's blades were the best the world had ever seen. The superior metallurgy and his secret techniques had seen Grendell become famous. The enemy had attacked the small town a number of times in an effort to capture him.

One day they returned, in greater numbers than ever before. Caught by surprise and heavily outnumbered, the menfolk fought bravely to protect their smith but it was no use, even with their superior blades. Grendell was tied up and carried off and the town would never see him again.

But Grendell knew this day would come and he had made preparations. The King had a note, one that should only be opened in the event of his capture. It contained instructions for a new type of sword, and the number that should be made.

With tears in his eyes, the King read the note and immediately ordered work to begin.

Grendell was taken deep into enemy territory and presented to their King.

"So this is the famous Grendell," he sneered. "Your work has seen many of my men killed. Now you will make swords for me. I want the very best from you, Grendell, or I will cut your throat myself."

Grendell was taken away, down into the bowels of the castle and his knees were smashed with a hammer. He would not be escaping this place.

He was given six weeks to recover from his hobbling, during which time his captors repelled a number of weak attacks. It was as though Grendell's people weren't really trying that hard to recapture him.

Grendell made a sword for his new King. It took weeks and the other smiths studied every part of the process in great detail. Grendell's secrets would be theirs. He moved slowly, his legs held together with wooden frames, and he was in a great deal of pain. He knew he would die here.

The King swung his new sword through one of the supporting stone columns of the council hall and the column shattered into a hundred pieces of rubble. A collective gasp went up from the attendant crowd.

The King held his new sword up to the light and saw that it was undamaged.

"You've done a good job, Grendell," he said. "This may be the finest sword ever made."

Grendell, watching from the side, bowed his head a touch.

"I want thirty thousand more, exactly like this," said the king. "Take as many men as you need. You have six months."

Six months later, the king had his swords. Grendell and his new aides had toiled day and night to make them on time. Everything was the same as the king's sword, including the secret additional ingredient **[1]** that would make the blade cut through stone, as the king had seen. Grendell had the power, it seemed, to make swords that were unbreakable.

Grendell's knowledge of metallurgy was unsurpassed and he received much praise from Danzing, who declared war on King Riordan and set a date for the battle on the open fields of the Middle Country.

There, two weeks later, the two great armies met. Both sides were certain of victory.

King Danzig knew that he would win because his swords were made by the blacksmith Grendell, the finest and most knowledgeable smith in the world.

King Riordan knew he would win because his opponent's swords were made by Grendell, his friend and loyal subject, and the finest and most knowledgeable smith in the world.

The two armies met on the field. Riordan's men charged on foot and on horseback and got themselves drenched scarlet with the enemy's blood right away. Their swords shone briefly in the sunlight before arcing down against the blades of their opponents.

At the first strike, the enemy blades shattered and were useless. Confused, screaming with rage and terror, Danzig's men were chopped up and cut down and the bloody field was soon littered with broken swords and body parts.

King Danzig fled before the end of the battle. King Riordan stood the victor and his men cheered loudly, but his was not the name they cheered.

"Grendell! Grendell!" went the cries. They all knew the sacrifice their smith had made for them. He would be remembered.

Grendell was on his knees, forced to remain there despite the agony this caused him. King Danzig paced back and forth in front of him, screaming obscenities, knowing his kingdom was lost and his reign at an end. Riordan would come and take the city. The rest of the country would soon fall.

"You did this!" said Danzig, pointing a finger at Grendell.

Grendell smiled and nodded.

"Your king will not rescue you. You will be dead a minute from now. Before I kill you, tell me how you did this to me."

Grendell laughed, not afraid of his impending death.

"I added a little something to your blades," he said, looking Danzig in the eyes. "Powerful enough to smash stone, yes, but brittle against a certain other ingredient **[2]**. And for my king – my true king – I left instructions to also make new swords. You should never have brought me here."

Danzig smiled grimly and reached for his sword. He held it up to the light and examined it one last time.

"This sword is only good for one thing," he said.

Grendell bowed his head, knowing what that one thing was.

And there is the story of my ancestor Grendell and the sacrifice he made to save his people. As far as I know it is a true story.

[1] *I cannot reveal the actual ingredient in my retelling of this story as my own business still relies on such secret knowledge.*

[2] *As* ***[1]****.*

Beautiful Eyes

I first saw her at a party. It was funny, because I had no intention of going and really didn't want to be there. To think, I might never have even met her. But I went, against my better judgement and within a few minutes I could sense that someone was watching me. Turning my head, it was as though nobody else in the world existed because my eyes found hers and our gaze locked.

A look like that is filled with terror, of wonder. A world of possibilities, a universe of potential. A look like that opens up your future and invites you to tread a previously unseen path.

I took that path. I'd have been mad not to. Eloise was the most beautiful girl I'd seen in a long, long time. Before her – years before – was Jane. And before her, Angelica. Helen. Yvonne. Of course, a man in my position – independently wealthy, well travelled, randomly gifted with good looks (through genes I'd inherited from my parents) – never has trouble finding attractive women to fool around with. I'm not saying they can smell wealth, but they can sense something different about people like me.

And I am different to most other men.

Eloise was so much more than the attractive creature that caught my attention, and from the moment I started talking to her I realised she was ferociously intelligent as well. The first ten minutes of conversation skimmed across the subjects of politics, of Capitalism, of the shared love of the Tuscan countryside in the Autumn. We danced around subjects, surprisingly in tune with each other. I remember nothing else about the party, only that I met Eloise there.

There was a lot I loved about her - from the way she wore her clothes, the way she walked, her innate sense of style without having to keep track of the latest trends. These are all physical things, which paints a distorted picture of my feelings for her. But I also loved the way she thought, the way she could utter a few choice words at the right moment to have me laughing so hard I'd get stitch. Most of all, though, I loved her eyes and the way she used to look at me.

Hazel irises, with flecks of green and the whole lot took on an amber lustre when the sunlight caught them. I could lose myself looking into her eyes. They were exotic and mysterious, like distant galaxies. Her gaze was sensual, suggestive yet restrained at the same time. Sometimes I felt like I was being observed by a wild creature. The hair on the back of my neck would rise and my body flushed with hormones brought on by the animal magnetism that filled a room whenever we were contained by four walls.

But these things don't last, unfortunately. Given a long enough timeline – about three years in our case – the cracks literally begin to appear. Before I am judged as shallow, let me state that Eloise was one of those women where the aging process only deepens their beauty. It was her mind that turned ugly. At the beginning there were moments of impatience, small things about me that frustrated her. There are things in any relationship that partners don't like about each other but they are pushed back, relegated into oblivion.

Eloise simply couldn't disregard my shortcomings.

At first there would be a small sigh whenever I did something that annoyed her. I would look across and she would follow the sigh with a quick grin, but after a while the grin stopped appearing. There would be a mutter under her breath, a quiet storming out of the room. God only knows, the number of things that annoyed her grew by the day.

At first it was my addiction to cigarellos, and then there was something about my clothes. She said I had begun snoring and sometimes couldn't bear sleeping in the same bed as me. Eventually, even a simple thing like my eating an apple would drive her mad. It was the noise of it, she said, but I ask you – who can eat an apple quietly?

Our arguments grew more frequent, more devastating. Once or twice she left and stayed at hotels. I tried, many times, to find out what was wrong but I could never get to the bottom of it. It was as though she hated me. I felt like the poor creature in Poe's 'The Black Cat', persecuted for showing unrequited affection when the narrator suddenly finds the adoration of his pet suddenly loathsome. I came to realise that Eloise loathed me. I never figured out why, only that she did.

It was too much to bear. No man can take such rejection. Even I, with a history of similar experiences, found this one more painful than the last. I was adrift in a lonely sea, and she seized upon my weakness and took it as an invitation to scorn me relentlessly, to diminish my masculinity at every opportunity. It was torture, each day more miserable than the previous ones, until I lost my centre.

This again, I said to myself. Why does this keep happening?

In situations like these, pushed to one's limit, the solution is obvious but one must commit to it.

Eloise always did have beautiful eyes, but the lustre has long faded. They were the only thing of hers I kept. Now they are all milky and the jar containing them needs a good clean. It is the same jar, incidentally, where I previously kept my mementoes of Jane, of Angelica and the rest. I can't quite bring myself to throw these bits of Eloise out yet, my love for her was so strong that to rid the Earth of her completely seems a step too far.

One day, I will take them to the secret place where I scattered her ashes and throw them down for the carrion but not yet.

Not yet, no.

Necro Orbis Terrarum

This is what we know. It spreads on the land, killing everything it touches. Nothing seems to be able to stop it. When it gets to water it spreads unevenly, surging with the unseen currents, and in the air there doesn't seem to be enough matter for it to get a hold – if you are close enough you can sometimes see it trying to catch, flowering patches of black that suddenly sprinkle back down to the ground.

It started in Cambridge. I know this because I was there. It's partly my fault. We sealed off the site but we weren't prepared and our safety precautions came to nothing. It got out. Like a stain spreading on a map, it grew in size until any thoughts of containment became impossible.

We abandoned the site and, later, we abandoned the country. Those that could get out were lucky – perhaps two million, flooding into Europe and further afield – and then the country was quarantined off and everyone left behind was doomed. That was 7 months ago. Britain is now cold and dead, an entire island made of black matter with nothing left alive. No vegetation, no animals, no people. Everything is gone.

Europe met the same fate months later, by which time the currents had taken the spread across the Atlantic and it was making progress across the eastern seaboard. The cities emptied and people fled west, like the days of the settlers following the railroads. Even as tens of millions were displaced, the blackness was spreading around Greenland and creeping down through Canada.

It was surging on multiple fronts and people were flocking to the areas where they thought they would be safest the longest. Nowhere was safe. It couldn't be stopped.

Across the world, the same carnage played out. Sea-ports and airports swamped with crowds of people, with no resources to sustain them whilst any exodus was administrated. Society breaking down. Hopelessness. Fighting. People in fear for their lives. People murdering each other as the shadow drew nearer. And then, when there was nowhere left to go, people throwing themselves into the sea in their thousands, drowning when they could swim no further.

So how did this happen? What caused the end of the world?

Curiosity and the need to understand. We were looking at the world on a quantum level and somewhere in the foam we found our doom. You'd think I was an astrophysicist or something but you'd be wrong. I was in charge of the Institute for Paranormal Research. We didn't do this with science – we did it with the mind. Specifically, the mind of M.A., a Belarusian woman with psychic abilities. Despite my position, I never really believed in that sort of thing – my job was essentially to disprove psychic phenomena and I'd always managed to do that.

Not this time.

We showed her a black dot on a sheet of paper and asked her to go smaller. Down to the microscopic level. Smaller, we asked her. Describe what you see. Down to the atomic level. Smaller than an electron. What do you see?

"Fuzz," she told us. "It's all fuzzy."

Quarks and leptons. Go smaller, we told her. She was sweating profusely with the effort of the journey. Within minutes she was describing things we couldn't even have imagined. Normally, people would smash particles together at close to the speed of light to get tantalising glimpses of the world at this scale but we achieved much more than this for the price of a cheap flight and plenty of cigarettes.

"I can see something else," she said, right at the end. "It is there and not there at the same time. I can feel it drawing me closer."

"Go closer," we told her.

"It hurts. I am not supposed to be seeing this. Nobody is."

"Go closer."

"Everything is slowing down. This thing, it looks like some sort of switch."

"What does that mean?"

"It's the only way to describe it. On or off."

"It's on, at the moment?"

"Yes."

The team discussed what we should do. We thought there would be no harm in interfering.

"Turn it off."

We didn't know that it would start turning off adjacent switches, and each one in turn would do the same. It grew exponentially. M.A. emerged from her trance, screaming, clutching at her head and within a minute the dot on the sheet was getting bigger. One of my team reached out to touch it and then he started screaming. A few minutes later he was dead, a black shape on the floor that was more a total absence of reflected light than anything real.

I don't know what happened to the rest of my colleagues. I don't know what happened to M.A.. All dead, I'd guess.

Now, I'm sitting halfway up a mountain somewhere in Borneo. For somewhere that was once so remote, it's now densely populated with people like myself, temporary survivors on a dying planet. We have a few days before it reaches us. There will be no escape but it's not stopping us from trying to live as long as we can. I've traversed three continents and killed a dozen people to get here and I'm ashamed of that but I'd do it again. I will kill again, before the end. I'll fight to be the last one on this mountain as the blackness spreads upwards and comes to claim me.

At the end of all this, Earth will be nothing more than a dead thing floating in space. We all knew that this was going to happen, one way or another. If there's one certainty in our destiny as a race it's our commitment to destruction. Whether we blew ourselves up, poisoned ourselves, destroyed the climate or maybe even created a grey-goo of nanobots it was always going to end this way.

Therapist

We had a hundred crime reports but none of them were any use. Details were always vague, as though none of the victims could remember a single thing about their attacker. We knew he was male, that was the only thing anyone could agree on. Some say dark hair, some say blonde. Bearded, clean shaven, tall, average height, green eyes, brown. We had numerous DNA samples but there was always a problem with the analysis and whenever you went looking for the results they seemed to have disappeared.

Our biggest lead – and it was a constant fight to stop that getting lost as well – was a grainy black and white photo taken from CCTV footage and sent in anonymously. It showed the grey figure of a man in the darkness with little other detail. It had been accompanied by a simple scrawled note: 'This is therapist'.

It had been ignored for months, almost thrown away a dozen times. Nobody knew what to make of it or what it meant. We thought that some therapy company had come up with a really weird marketing campaign.

I connected it to the case one day during a rare moment when my foggy thoughts seemed to clear for a few seconds.

There had been over a hundred attacks across the southeast region, possibly double that number. Women, mostly, but also a handful of men. Attacked from behind, beaten into compliance before being held down and raped, sometimes bundled in the boot of a car and driven somewhere quiet first.

I'd been tasked to the case for five months and progress had been slow. More honestly, non-existent. It was slowly sending me over the edge – whenever we got the tiniest wisp of information it always seemed to peter out to nothing. And I kept stumbling across this photo, constantly resisting the urge to just throw it away. And then, one day, clarity. This is the rapist. The scrawled note, the tiniest of gaps between the 'e' and the 'r' that we'd missed, again and again.

The fact that we have this bastard in custody has nothing to do with that note, or our investigative work on the case. He was picked up for a traffic violation and there was a trussed-up woman in his boot. He hadn't tried to fight or get away.

"Get in there and interview the fucker," said DI Fisk, looking my way. He was old-school, an ex-military man with a grey crew cut and arms like Popeye. He'd have liked nothing more that to get in there and beat the shit out of him.

I entered the interview room and sat down opposite our man. I looked at him for a good minute, taking in his features, but if you asked me to describe him for you now I wouldn't be able to. I think he had dark hair but I couldn't be sure. For a few moments I forgot why I was even there, or what I was supposed to be doing. My thoughts had fogged and I couldn't seem to get myself together. Somehow, just being in the presence of this man was throwing my brain out of whack.

A few minutes later I found myself back outside with Fisk, with no memory of the interview.

"Well?" asked Fisk.

"Well, what?"

"Did you get anything out of him?"

I struggled to remember anything. I couldn't.

"Didn't you see on the cameras?" I asked, avoiding the question.

"They're playing up – picture keeps rolling and the audio's fucked. So, you didn't get anything out of him?"

I shook my head apologetically. Fisk's face creased with anger.

"I want some time with him," he said.

"Do you want me to come back in with you?"

"No. Just keep everyone else out of the way. And turn the cameras off completely."

He'd done this a couple of times before. Both times the suspects had come out the other side considerably the worse for wear.

"No problem," I said.

I went back to my desk, grabbing a coffee from the machine on the way. I sat and waited, wondering what Fisk would do to him, how far he would go. Who the hell was this man we had in there? It was as though he moved through the world jamming the thoughts of everyone around him. We still knew nothing about him – the car we picked him up in had been stolen and he had no ID.

After ten minutes turned into fifteen I went back to the interview room and the door was ajar. Inside, Fisk was lying crumpled in a corner of the room, sobbing and naked from the waist down. There was a smear of blood on the interview desk and on his inner thighs. I looked around but there was nobody there with him.

"Are you all right?" I asked, bending down next to him.

"Get away from me!" he snarled, lashing out with his arm and looking at me with the frightened eyes of a child.

I backed away and ran out of the room, calling out for help. My colleagues started rushing over asking what was wrong.

"Have you seen our suspect?" I shouted. "Did you see him leave the interview room?"

People looked at each other, confused.

"What does he look like?" someone asked.

I couldn't answer. I didn't know.

I raced to the reception area and saw that the door was wide open. Our civilian staff receptionist Wendy, a sweet old dear coming up to retirement age, was sitting there with a grin on her face. She looked at me like she was just coming out of a dream.

We never found him. Although we'd turned off the cameras in the interview room, the rest were left on and even though they kept rolling and freezing we managed to get a shot of our man as he left the station. It was a man from the back, a grey figure against a dark background, much like the other picture.

It could have been anyone.

Blowing in the Wind

Dear Marie,

I will be dead when you read this. This short letter is my goodbye to you. You have been a dear friend and my life has been easier with you in it.

Thank you.

Please find below precise instructions for my funeral and a list of people to invite. The box accompanying this letter contains an item for every person on the list. Please ensure that all of my instructions are followed exactly.

Finally, there is a sealed letter for Drwal – please deliver to him, by hand, one month after my body has been burnt.

Hopefully there is an afterlife and I will see you there.

Your good friend,

Tomas

Marie sobbed as she read the letter for perhaps the hundredth time.

Poor Tomas. He'd never been the same since he met Drwal. Thirty years ago, their paths had crossed and Drwal had become a benefactor, offering free office space and help bringing his inventions to fruition. And then Drwal had stolen everything. He had grown rich, exploiting Tomas's talent, using his connections to block every attempt at legal recourse.

Sometimes great men are hounded by a nemesis who make it their life's work to bring doom to the other. Darwin and Owen, Poe and Griswold, Tesla and Edison. Even though Tomas was down on his luck for most of his life, Drwal never resisted the urge to put the boot in as often as he could.

Whilst Drwal grew rich and moved in high circles, Tomas struggled to avoid the gutter and took menial work to stay afloat. One of the greatest scientific minds the world had seen spent time cleaning toilets for minimum wage and blew a good deal of what he earned on cheap liquor.

Marie had saved him. She pulled him from the verge of homelessness and utter despair and gave him a place to live. With her help, he came back from the brink and almost became the man he once was. He found a good job and eventually moved out to a place of his own. They remained close friends.

The funeral was a humanist ceremony. The body was placed on top of a six-foot pyre, very specifically sited according to Tomas' instructions. At this place, the wind always blew south-east.

There were exactly twenty mourners. Each was given a tiny box and a note. Inside the box was Tomas' final invention. Before being taken to the ceremony Marie ensured that they were correctly positioned and the note gave specific instructions on how the mourners should conduct themselves throughout.

Shortly before the pyre was lit, an uninvited figure showed up and stood to one side. Dressed in a long black Mackintosh, Drwal sneered at the people who had come to pay their final respects to Tomas. He looked at the dead body atop the pyre and felt nothing.

It had always been so easy to put Tomas down, he was such a hopeless victim. He'd had some good ideas but hadn't a clue how to progress them forward – weak men like Tomas would never change the world. This weakness disgusted Drwal and as time went by he found him even more loathsome. Tomas had wilted under life's pressures and never had the gumption to mount any counter-attack worthy of note. Drwal wouldn't have minded a good fight, legal or otherwise, but Tomas couldn't even manage that.

Perhaps, somewhere deep and forgotten, there was guilt and a need to see Tomas wiped from the Earth so the fear of discovery that his own life's work was based on stolen ideas would forever be eradicated. More than that, though, Drwal mostly wanted to see Tomas wiped away because he was bored with him.

The pyre was lit and the mourners watched in silence. Drwal watched as the flames leapt towards the body as if drawn to it, eager to consume the flesh and turn the corpse to ash. Nobody spoke, there was no eulogy. The wooden structure crackled and popped, the dark suit around Tomas began to smoulder. In moments, the pale flesh of his hands and face began to darken and his grey hair caught alight and sizzled away to nothing.

Thick smoke coiled upwards and, caught by the steady wind, blew down across the mourners. Drwal coughed, caught in a rancid cloud, conscious of the fact that the fumes he breathed were once part of Tomas. He hacked up a great wodge of phlegm and spat it onto the ground and then, having seen enough, he turned and left.

A month later, Drwal lay across his sofa, his flesh grey and waxen. He seemed to have aged twenty years and his body was racked with coughing fits and painful spasms.

He was disturbed by a ringing of the doorbell and slowly heaved himself upright and shuffled to the front door. A woman he vaguely knew stood there, holding out a letter.

"What is this?" said Drwal, looking around the street behind her.

"I was instructed to deliver this to you personally," she said. "Take it."

Drwal slowly reached out and took the letter and the woman immediately walked away. He closed the door and returned to the lounge, coughing. He sat down and opened it.

Drwal,

You are dying. I have caused this. Consider it my revenge.

The week before my death I consumed small quantities of xxxx. It slowly poisoned me, the way it now poisons you. I knew you would come to my funeral to gloat, and I knew that you would breathe my fumes. One property of xxxx is that it becomes even more toxic when burned.

You will want to know why my friends are not dying alongside you. My final, and perhaps my greatest invention, was the smallest – a simple breatheable nose-plug to filter out the fumes. Everyone that was invited wore one.

You were not, and did not. I leave you now to your own slow and painful death.

You deserve this.

Regards,

Tomas

Volume 3

The Fly
Timothy's Terrible Trump
Change
Cordyceps
I'll Meet You at the Top of the Tower
Who's the Boss Now?
Two Magpies
Clit Hero
WC Blues
The Joke
Anti-Claus
Glitter

The Fly

The gym I go to is full of hi-tech equipment and city types lifting mini dumbbells and getting an hour on the cross-trainer either side of work. I've been going there about five years and I hardly recognise three-quarters of the people around me. I remember the old days, when it was the more hardcore types, grunting as they bench-pressed four hundred kilograms and the whole place stank of sweat and Ralgex.

Back then most of the gym-bunnies couldn't walk properly, their upper torsos were so wide they walked around with their arms splayed, careful not to bump into each other for fear of provoking a roid-rage incident.

There aren't many of those types left now. In fact there's just the one. His name is Duke. That's obviously not his real name but nobody calls him out on it. Duke's a gorilla, a three hundred pound mass of muscle loaded with testosterone and meanness. I once saw him rip a door off its hinges when someone knocked over one of his protein shakes by accident. They've tried to ban him from the gym but he just keeps coming back. I think they're too scared to try and enforce the ban and just hope that he remains calm and nobody upsets him. He's a goddamned bully.

I prefer things like the running and rowing machines to lifting weights. I'm fit and strong but hardly a poster boy for exercise. I don't have a six-pack or anything and I don't take it too seriously. I'm not afraid to eat and drink what I like, and coming to the gym three times a week seems to hold off the lard from my belly.

Take today, for instance. After work I went for a meal with some of the guys from the office and had my fill of chicken and pasta, all washed down with a beer. I even had a bit of a colleague's raw fish and wasabi sauce. I tell you, that stuff is hot. I had to excuse myself to go and wash the tears from my eyes and stood there hunched over one of the sinks in the toilets heaving, thinking I was going to puke. What the hell do they put in wasabi? How can a food sauce be so painful?

Afterwards, I drove home and watched a bit of television before getting changed and heading down to the gym. It had been a really hot summer day, touching the thirties, and the gym was still humid. With the amount of cleaning fluid and polish the owners dash about the place it's not often the smell of stale sweat rises up and overpowers everything else but it stank in there.

I nodded hello to a few faces I recognised and even before I saw him I heard Duke grunting away on some bit of equipment on the other side of the large room. I took a seat in a rower and started working out.

A big bluebottle kept circling and threatening to land on my face. It had been hanging around the gym for days and I was surprised that it hadn't found its way out through a window. What on earth had it been eating? I kept blowing air at it every time it circled my head but it kept coming back, putting me right off my routine. I glanced across at Big Jim on one of the cycling machines and he smirked at me.

"Fly bothering you?" he asked.

“Yeah.”

“Why don’t you kill it?”

“Why don’t *you* kill it?”

“I’m working out here.”

“And I’m not?”

“Yeah, but it ain’t bothering me as much as it’s bothering you.”

He was right. After it landed on my head a second time I stood up and swatted the air. I'd had enough of this fly. If no-one else was going to deal with it then I would. I looked around and walked over to the reception counter to pick up some fitness promotional magazine before rolling it up and going on the hunt.

I stalked it around the gym, baton ready to smash it to smithereens. I followed it around the large room, totally engrossed in killing the little fucker. I didn't take my eyes off that fly and still managed to navigate my way between the bits of machinery and people going about their business of improving themselves. Eventually, I found myself on the far side of the room and was within a few feet of it. I raised my arm and got ready to swing.

The fly landed on something pink and shiny, some dim fixture within the focus of my glare. I was consumed, blessed with tunnel vision. With a shout of "Hah!" I swung the baton down as hard as I could and connected against something with a loud BAM!

I must have got it. I looked around the gym with a big grin to find everyone had stopped training to look at me. It had gone very quiet in there. I turned back. The pink shiny thing I'd just whacked turned out to be the top of Duke's big bald head. The fly was smeared across his scalp.

He stood and towered over me. His face was turning purple with anger. A little fart squeaked out of my shorts. I was done for. I could see murder in his eyes. He looked at me for a very long time, his fists clenching and unclenching and I waited for him to pound me through the wall.

Instead, his face crumpled and he burst into tears. I couldn't believe it. With a girlish shriek, he ran towards the toilet block and disappeared inside. Everyone in the gym was looking at me as though I was some sort of god.

I learned a valuable lesson about bullies that day. I also learned to never eat wasabi sauce again. And, if you ever want anything doing, don’t bother asking Big Jim.

Timothy's Terrible Trump

Timothy awoke with a pain in his guts, as though he'd swallowed a bowling ball in the night. He sat on the end of his bed and groaned. Something wasn't right. He had the most overwhelming urge to break wind but knew that he mustn't. It had been a very long time since he'd last trumped. Bad things happened when Timothy trumped.

When Timothy was a baby, his father had been changing his nappy one day and Timothy did a bottom burp that was so powerful it blew his father's moustache right off his face. His father looked everywhere and eventually found it hiding under the television cabinet, shivering with fright.

Another time, whilst his mother was pushing him along in his pram, Timothy guffed and the pram flew out of his mother's grasp and hurtled down the street at a hundred miles per hour.

And there was that incident with the nun and her wimple that was better left unmentioned. But after that, and as soon as he could understand words, Timothy's mother and father warned him that he should never break wind again because disaster was never far behind.

For eight years, Timothy had not trumpeted from his backside, not even a tiny parp. Through pre-school and junior school, whenever he felt the need he'd held it in. Finally, after all these years of holding things in, the pressure had built up to such an extent that Timothy was fit to explode.

At breakfast, he couldn't eat.

"Are you OK, Timmy?" asked his mom.

Timothy smiled, concentrating on trying not to break wind.

In the car on the way to school, he fidgeted in his seat.

In his first lesson, his stomach ache grew so bad that he almost cried.

Out in the playground, as all of his friends ran around after a football, Timothy knew that he couldn't hold on any longer. The urge was becoming unbearable. He wondered if it wouldn't be so bad if he just let a little one out – surely nobody would notice a tiny bottom squeak and, if nobody did, maybe he could keep letting little ones out for the rest of the day until the pressure eased?

He decided to risk it. He closed his eyes and trumped.

As soon as he started he knew he'd made a terrible mistake. It wouldn't stop! The tiny squeak in his trousers grew into a rumble and then surged into a mighty roar. It was like an earthquake! The ground shook. The school windows shattered. All of his friends were knocked over. The football was blasted into the next county. Birds fell from the sky. Bushes and trees were stripped of their leaves.

And then it was over and a great silence descended as the world tried to make sense of what had just happened. Everybody looked at Timothy, shocked. The silence didn't last for very long. Car alarms started going off. People shouted and ran screaming in all directions. Dogs barked and cats howled. Suddenly, there was noise everywhere!

And then the unimaginable happened.... the smell came, wrapped in a rapidly expanding, murky brown cloud. It was a proper stinker. His friends rolled around on the ground, coughing and crying. Plants wilted. The grass turned brown. Inside the school, the teachers keeled over and fainted. Never was there such an abominable smell in all of history.

The cloud spread, an evil miasma that started to block out the sun, a vaporous nebula of guff-gas that seemed to give everything a sticky coating. It spread through the streets, across the parks, into the shopping centres and industrial estates. Builders stopped building, dropping to their knees in fits of coughing. People stumbled around the malls in a daze, walking outside to gasp in horror at the premature night. Drivers put on their fog lights and were forced to stop. Roads became blocked. Motorways came to a standstill. The entire country ground to a halt!

School was cancelled and all of the children were sent home. Timothy walked through the foggy streets, looking at all of the carnage he'd caused. Crashed cars, dead trees, old people being taken to hospitals in ambulances. There were frightened cats, terrified dogs and birds splattered all over the pavements where they'd tumbled from the sky. And it was all his fault!

If only he hadn't given into the urge to let one go. But it was too late for regrets.

He walked home, his cheeks burning with shame. All the way he was accompanied by the shouts and howls of people and animals in despair. It felt like the world itself was ending, that civilisation was collapsing. Timothy didn't know much about history but he knew that many different empires had come and gone and sometimes there was no way of explaining their disappearance. Maybe there were other trumpers in history, people just like himself who caused empires to fall simply by emitting the most devastating parps and people weren't strong enough to recover from the carnage.

At home that night, Timothy watched the television with his parents. Normal programs had been replaced by a rolling newscast. The country was in chaos. Even the newsreader was wearing a gasmask. There was lots of video of brown fog covering various cities. Planes had been grounded and businesses had lost billions of pounds as no trading could continue under the circumstances. There was talk of the military declaring martial law. And then, just before the end of the news, there was a power-cut and everything went dark.

His mother tucked him into bed. If she knew that Timothy was the cause of all this chaos, she didn't say anything about it. Instead, as a candle flickered on the bedside table, she asked how his stomach was.

"A little better," said Timothy.

His mother kissed him on the forehead and said goodnight before leaving the room. Timothy lay awake, thinking about the day's events.

I'm never going to trump again, he thought to himself.

And he never did.

Change

21-SEP

Ah walked down by the shopping centre, where the new road-works are blocking all the traffic. All the cones were just dumped there. Not even in a straight line. It's been doin' mah nut in for weeks. I couldnae take it no more, ah had to measure them out properly. Sixteen paces between each one, and then one pace perpendicular from the kerb. Ah had shit from all the cars stopping as I went about this task, and then someone called the polis. Ah knows the polis, they know I have to keep the world ordered by now. They moved me on.

22-SEP

Ah bought a chocolate bar from the garage, one o' they ones with the dark chocolate. Red wrapper. Ah paid and for some reason didnae count ma change as ah was walkin' away. Mebbe distracted by the impending chocolate. Later, when ah counted ma change, ah was 5p short.

23-SEP

"Youse ripped me off!" ah telt him. Ah wanted my change but this little prick wouldnae listen. I telt him, yesterday he gave me short-change but he pretended not tae know what ah'm on about. The manager got involved an' everythin'. Said if ah didnae turn it down a bit ah'd end up banned from every garage north of Hawick.

Ah left 'em to it. But ah'm not havin' that. Ah'm gonna go in there every day from now on and buy a chocolate bar and count ma change until that little prick does me again. Then ah'll have the radge bastard.

24-SEP

Ah bought a chocolate bar. Correct change.

25-SEP

Ah bought a chocolate bar. Correct change.

26-SEP

The little prick wasnae behind the counter. It's his day off. Ah bought a chocolate bar anyways. Correct change.

27-SEP

He's not there today either! Radge bastard. Ah bought a chocolate bar. Correct change.

28-SEP

He's back! Ah bought a chocolate bar. Correct change. He knows ah'm onto him. Ah need to mix it up a bit.

29-SEP

Ah didnae buy a chocolate bar. Take that ya prick! Ah buys a pack ay crisps, on offer, and pay the radge. He gives me short change. Ah kick off.

"YA WEE PRICK!" ah screams at him. "Ah fuckin' knew ya'd do me again! Youse picked on the wrong man, ah'm fuckin' havin' youse for this one!"

The manager comes out again and asks me to calm down.

"CALM DOWN?" ah yells. "With this prick doin' me over?"

They have some discussion and the manager tells me ah'm in the wrang. He gets me to look at the offer label on the crisp shelf and ah see that the crisps ah've bought aren't the ones on offer. Ah fuckin' mixed mysen up not buyin' that chocolate!

30-SEP

Ah bought a chocolate bar. Ah'm not givin' up on this. Correct change.

01-OCT

There's a new crack in the pavement outside the SPAR shop. Ah draw it in ma notebook. These things need trackin'. Forgot to buy a chocolate bar.

02-OCT

Ah bought a chocolate bar. The radge gis ma change all in pennies. His smile soon disappears when ah insist on countin' it all out before I move out of the way for the next customer. Ah had to count it three times before ah was happy ah'd not been ripped off. Fuckin' wideboy thinks he can get one o'er me? Not a chance.

03-OCT

It's his day off again. Ah know he's not doing it deliberately but it's really messin' up ma system wi' him not being there all the time. How am ah supposed to monitor this shite when the variables keep changin'?

04-OCT

He's not there again. Ah didnae see the point of buyin' any more of that fuckin' chocolate, which ah'm beginning to hate almost as much as the cunt that's been sellin' me them. Av've stopped eatin' the shite. On the way back home, ah check on that crack outside the SPAR and it's no different. Most of the time they never are. The one ah tracked outside the library took three years before it got any bigger.

05-OCT

The radge is back. He groaned when he saw me. Ah'm getting' to him. Little did he know when he ripped me off that ah'd be in this for the long haul! They never do! Ah've done this before, see, and ah always win. Ah bought a chocolate bar and I stared into his eyes. I telt him, through my mind: *Ah've your number.* Correct change.

06-OCT

Ah bought a chocolate bar. Correct change.

07-OCT

Ah bought a chocolate bar. Correct change. He's getting' some ay his confidence back. No more groanin' from this prick, he's playin' the game now. We both know ah'm comin' in here until one of us cracks. Ah know ah'm not crackin' first.

08-OCT

Ah bought a chocolate bar. The radge gis me too much change, by 5p. There was this look on his face, something like *'Ah've gid ya an extra 5p now fuck off and leave me alone!'*. He's confused me now. Ah wasnae expectin' this development. Ah go home and mull it over for the rest of the day.

09-OCT

Ah bought a chocolate bar. Big sigh from him. Correct change.

10-OCT

Radge not there again. Ah knew he wouldna be. I know his work pattern now an' he'll be off tomorrow as well. No chocolate today. Ah've a big pile of the bastard things at home anyways.

11-OCT

Radge not there – ah checked anyway.

12-OCT

Radge not there again! What's this? I ask to see the manager. He telt me the cashier has quit his job an' won't be comin' back. The manager looked at me funny, as though he was gonna say somethin' else but he doesnae. Ah'm stuck now. The short change situation cannae have a resolution.

13-OCT

Ah took all ma spare chocolate back for a refund. The manager's fuckin' banned me! What the fuck is wrang with some people?

Cordyceps

The Fungal Research and Development Centre is a collection of buildings tucked away in the Berkshire countryside, primarily funded by the government but also receptive to corporate requests from any companies that are prepared to pay a premium for the resources. Although nobody at the centre would openly admit it, even if they actually knew about it, there were also military interests.

Tad Brenneman led a small team that had, for the last two years, been studying the effects of the *Ophiocordyceps unilateralis*, a particularly nasty fungus that had recently attracted a lot of attention when images of infected ants were posted on various websites and subsequently went viral. This, despite the fact that the fungus had been quietly going about the same distressing business for just under 50 million years. The images showed ants, quite dead, with a column of sprouting fungus emerging from their heads.

Gruesome enough, but what really caused a sensation was the fact that the fungus actually controlled the ants in the stages leading up to their eventual demise, causing them to climb trees to gain optimum height for the sprouting fungus to eventually explode and ensure maximum distribution when spreading. It seemed incredible that a mere fungus could intelligently control another organism in this manner, and despite the natural world being rife with examples of similarly 'intelligent' parasitic behaviour, this is the one that seemed to catch the public's interest.

Tad and his team were trying to unlock the mysteries of the parasitic process. Studying ants in various stages of infection was a time-consuming, elaborate and expensive endeavour. It's not easy tracking changes in an ant's brain, and the necessary equipment costs were astronomical. For this reason, Tad's team had been experimenting with ways to mutate the fungus so that it would replicate the parasitic behaviour in larger creatures, ones that were already well understood from decades of familiarity with the laboratory: rats. So far, so good. Test subjects were demonstrating recognisable symptoms – confusion, extreme thirst and a compulsion to climb any high object.

Tad's lab and office area took up the entire ground floor of 'D' block, a five story red-brick building on the eastern edge of the complex. There were three other staff on his team, all of them easy-going academic types with a sense of humour even quirkier than their wardrobes. Work was winding down for Christmas, just over a week away.

Tad's day was not going well. There seemed to be yet another problem with the software controlling the population counts. It kept flashing up a warning that one of the test subjects was missing. Nobody took these seriously anymore after numerous errors in the past. This particular time, however, the software was functioning correctly. Nobody yet realised an infected rat had chewed its way through one of the cages and had found its way up into the false ceiling and expired. It had distributed spores just a few feet away from the air-conditioning exhaust.

"Anybody seen Jeff?" asked Tad. Jeff was the software nerd.

Alex shook his head and mumbled something. Smithers glanced up from his work and nodded towards the door.

"I saw him at the water cooler a few minutes ago."

Tad was just about to go looking for him when the desk phone rang. He picked up the receiver.

"Hello?"

"Hi Tad," said a voice on the other end. Tad recognised it as Julia in Archiving, up on the third floor. "Can you come and sort Jeff out please? He's acting weird."

"What kind of weird?"

"Just... weird."

"Where is he – with you guys?"

"He was, but I think he's up on the roof now."

Tad's stomach lurched. What was Jeff doing on the roof? Nobody ever went up there. He didn't like the sound of any of this. He told Julia he'd be right up and placed the handset down onto the cradle.

A few minutes later, Tad walked through the open exit door and stepped out onto the roof. Behind, Alex and Smithers hung back on the stairwell.

Jeff was standing at the very edge of the roof, hunched over with his back to Tad.

"Jeff?" he asked, cautiously stepping forward.

At the sound of Tad's voice, Jeff slowly turned around and his head came into view. His face was contorted beyond recognition. From the top of his head, a thick column of grey fungus was sprouting.

Cordyceps.

Tad turned to shout at the others. "Get this place locked down, right now – full emergency mode. Initiate the quarantine sequence." They fled back downstairs and he turned to face Jeff once more. Jeff's head twitched and his lips were curled back as far as they would go. Any sense of Jeff-ness was long gone – this thing standing before him no longer seemed human. It turned around in small, jerky movements. It teetered at the edge.

"Jeff?" he said in a quiet voice. "Can you hear me?

The thing tilted its head as though listening. Tad had no idea what to say. His mouth was dry and no words were forthcoming. He realised that he could really use a drink. He could almost sense each of the water coolers dotted throughout the building below him. For some reason, the thought of going back down disturbed him.

He stood and watched, his thoughts clouding, as the fungal column rising from the top of Jeff's head throbbed with some internal mechanism about to reach critical mass. Jeff suddenly launched himself into the air and, at the moment gravity claimed him, the column exploded with a soft *PFFFT!* sound and a cloud of spores was taken away by the wind.

Tad's last rational thought, which occurred to him just as the top of his skull started to crack, was that he wouldn't be making it home in time for Christmas this year.

I'll Meet You at the Top of the Tower

They were too young, the first time around. Meeting in their penultimate year at school, when her parents moved into the area on account of a new job, she walked into his French class one day and he was smitten. After a few months of barely being noticed, he suddenly walked up to her and asked her to go to the cinema with him and, out of surprise more than anything else, she agreed.

Out of school, alone, she discovered this boy with the same quirky sense of humour as her own. He was generous, kind, funny and, now that she had noticed him, good-looking in an understated way. They began an intense two year relationship and for a long time they were very happy. They thought they were in love.

Perhaps it was the intensity that eventually drove them apart, perhaps it was nothing more than starting off too young, whilst they were still growing, still developing their personalities, their eventual characters. She began to find him a little overbearing, his jokes less funny. He was needy and relied on her too much. He was prone to moodiness and often immature. She felt smothered.

They argued more frequently, culminating in a huge row the day she received a letter confirming a place at university. She would be moving hundreds of miles away and she simply came out and told him that she wanted to make a clean break of it. Afterwards, they didn't see each other – or even talk to each other – for months. On the day she was due to leave, she phoned his house and asked him to meet her at the top of the tower.

You could see the tower from miles away, especially at night when it was all lit up. He'd taken her there, once, for dinner in the top floor restaurant on her sixteenth birthday. He'd saved up for weeks to be able to afford it.

During the months apart, she'd softened a little. Away from him, she'd had time to reflect upon the good times they'd shared. She didn't want it to end this way, with animosity.

She was already sitting at a table when he entered the restaurant on the top floor. Her heart quickened a little upon seeing him. They ordered a light lunch and she asked him to go outside, onto the observation deck that circumvented the restaurant. There, leaning against the railing and looking down across a view of the entire county laid out before them, she made the suggestion.

Whatever happens, we'll meet here when we're thirty years old. On his birthday. If neither of them were in a relationship they would get married. He listened to the proposal in silence and then looked at her with a stunned expression.

It was something she'd seen in a soppy romantic movie one night when she was feeling low. It seemed like the right thing to do. It would give them time to grow, live their lives and see the world before, if nothing much happened in the intervening years, they could meet up and try again. A little older, a little wiser. To her relief, he agreed. They enjoyed lunch and with a single kiss, they parted.

The following years were good to her. She passed her degree, quickly found a well paid job and took up an interest in local theatre, at first working behind the scenes on a voluntary basis in her spare time and then, in a small emergency one night, heading out onto the stage to play a minor role with no more than a couple of lines. She found she loved acting and quickly became a valuable member of the cast.

She had her fair share of boyfriends, some serious, most not. She married, spent four years in what she believed to be a perfect relationship and then divorced after discovering her husband's many infidelities. She was promoted and then knocked for six when shortly afterwards the company declared itself on the verge of bankruptcy and folded. She used the opportunity to go travelling, and spent six months seeing the Far East.

Her life was well lived. In all that time, she barely thought of him.

His life took a darker path. His moody moments turned into darker fits of anger and despair and, as a twenty-first birthday present, he received a diagnosis for clinical depression. Shortly afterward he was declared bipolar.

He argued with his parents, lashing out whenever they uncharitably ordered him to 'pull himself together'. In the end they threw him out and he squatted in an abandoned building for a while. Sometimes, he slept in the park, or on the streets. Once, he became embroiled in an argument with a tramp and hit him on the head with a brick. He suspected he might have killed him, but didn't know for sure.

He knew his life was a mess but, whatever he did to try and steer it back on course, it never worked out. A black cloud seemed to follow him around. It was all her fault. Everything started to go wrong as soon as she left him. He started to hate her.

The years passed by. His thirtieth birthday loomed ever closer.

He was out on the observation deck when she arrived. Trying to hide how shocked she felt at the sight of him, she forced a smile and walked outside to say hello.

With one look, he felt the familiar rage growing inside. Before she'd even finished saying a greeting, he scooped her up and, with a howl of anger, launched her over the side of the railing. Screaming all the way, her mind trying desperately to process what was happening to her, she hurtled a thousand feet to her death and literally exploded upon hitting the pavement.

There were shouts and screams from inside the restaurant.

Looking at the people, surveying the world and everything in it with complete disdain, he climbed over the railing and launched himself after her.

Who's The Boss Now?

It should have been a sad day when George Pelham passed away but most of the people who might have missed him were already dead themselves. That's the thing about reaching a ripe old age – with every passing year, more contemporaries kick the bucket and one finds oneself in an ever-decreasing pool of friends until you're the last man standing and everyone else is dead. When that happens, the rest of the world doesn't care one way or the other.

By some miracle, his wife Frances had also managed to stay alive well into old age, a fact that had irked George because he couldn't stand the bitch. He used to love her, of course, but that was so long ago he couldn't even remember the decade when he realised he actually hated her. Always nagging, always moaning about something or other. It was his own fault for trying to please her in those early years, doing whatever she asked of him, never complaining. But, by the end, she simply bossed him around and he didn't have the fight in him to argue.

At the funeral director's place, three days after George's death, Frances stood by the till clutching her purse with her claw-like, arthritis riddled hands, waiting for the final bill. She'd had to catch the bus, now that George wasn't here to drive her around any more, and she cursed him every second of the journey. Still, the old bastard would be six feet under soon and she could spend her last few years as a happy old widow. She might even take on a younger lover, some whippersnapper in his sixties or early seventies, and fritter away their savings on fruit machines and bingo.

The funeral parlour was an unusual set-up, with three of the four walls of the main room containing a number of embedded glass tanks. Inside, various animals crawled or slept or sat watching her.

"Mrs Pelham," said Mendip the proprietor. "How are we today?" A small, thin man of Indian descent, he bowed slightly to Mrs Pelham to indicate his respect.

“Just get on with it,” she snapped, wanting to get the whole thing over with.

“Very well. But, before you settle up, can I interest you in our ‘Switch’ programme? Very reasonable rates for what you’re getting, if I say so myself.”

“No, thank you.”

“So you don’t want your husband back?”

“Back? What do you mean, ‘back’? He’s bloody dead.”

She looked at Mendip with glittering, beady eyes and wondered just what in the hell he was getting at. Bloody immigrant. You would never have had this nonsense with an English person running things.

“Haven’t you been keeping up with technological advances, Mrs Pelham?” asked Mendip, smiling and showing a row of tiny white teeth. “For a small fee, we can bring Mr Pelham back to you in the shell of any of these creatures you see all around us.” With a sweep of his arm, he gestured to the surrounding glass tanks.

Frances’s eyes narrowed with suspicion. She took a step towards one wall and inspected the creatures within the tanks. There was a large tarantula in one. A budgerigar in another. A snake. A kitten. A small dog. What was this, a funeral parlour or a bloody pet shop?

“You’re telling me,” she said, turning back to Mendip, “that my blasted George can come back as a spider? Or a bleedin’ budgie?”

“That is quite correct.”

“How does it work?”

“We have a licensed machine that can collect all the necessary information from the synapse map within his brain. It’s quite a marvellous creation. We transpose this into the creature of your choice. It’s all very elegant.”

“But he’s been dead three days.”

“It doesn’t matter, the process can work up to a week after death, if the brain is kept in optimum condition. Which, of course, it has.”

She stood for a moment or two, deliberating. It was tempting. Just when he thought he’d bloody escaped, she could have him back and have a moan at all the things she ran out of time to before the old sod popped his clogs. Yes, that was very tempting.

"How much do you want?" she asked.

"Oh, the price is very reasonable."

Two hours later, a small Chihuahua sat on the bus seat next to Frances looking bewildered. Same bloody expression George used to have on his face all the time, she thought. It was him all right.

"Just you wait 'til I get you home," she warned it. "You might be thinking you've got it made, having another chance at life, but you've got it all wrong. You're going to be the most miserable dog that ever lived, mark my words."

The dog looked at her without blinking. It could understand every word she said. Somewhere deep inside, George was already making plans. For the last twenty-five years, he'd been banging a lonely widow in the next street and she'd not long ago lost her own little dog. George knew he could get a bit of food and comfort there whenever he wanted. Frances could make all the threats she wanted, he had her number.

At their bus stop, Frances dragged the Chihuahua off the bus and along the pavement towards the house. George didn't much like being on a lead, much less when Frances felt like yanking it to make him walk faster. By the time they arrived home, George was in a bad mood like never before.

Inside, Frances unhooked the lead and started shouting at him. Ignoring her, George trotted straight into the lounge. When she followed, she found the little creature squatting over her best rug, a small swirl of fresh dung already out and steaming.

Frances's face was a picture.

"Why, you little..." she said, stepping towards him.

George's growl stopped her dead in her tracks. He may have been small but he made up for it with a newfound ferociousness.

"Oh, dear," said Frances. "Perhaps this wasn't such a good idea after all."

Clit Hero

Sam Perkins was sitting at his desk one day, idly daydreaming about what he was going to be getting up to with his new girlfriend that night, when the idea that would eventually make him a multi-millionaire struck him so hard it almost made him fall off his chair. Grabbing a pen and a notebook, he furiously scribbled down some notes and straight after booked a pitch slot for the following Monday. He spent the rest of the week putting together a presentation. As long as he kept up with his usual workload, the company would be fine with him using their resources for his own ideas. They encouraged it, in fact.

Sam worked for a software developer, one with a reputation for risk-taking. It was common practice for staff from any area to pitch an idea to management, however random. In the past, some of the more obscure ideas had made the company a lot of money, particularly in the Japanese market. If an idea was picked up and turned into a successful product, the originator of the idea would be cut in for a small percentage, regardless of their position on the payroll.

The developer, although a heavyweight, was much admired in the industry for its more independent approach to things, particularly with regard to the way it treated staff. As long as the work was done, they could do more or less what they liked. It was a *quid pro quo* arrangement – during the end of a game's development, the intense period of debugging and finalising that was known as 'crunch time', staff often worked 18 hour days without complaint.

The following Monday, after a weekend at home spent working on the pitch, Sam waited for his 3pm slot to arrive. When ready, he grabbed a free coffee from the machine and walked into the large meeting room. Six of the managers were waiting for him.

"Hey, Sam," said one, followed by greetings from the others.

"Hey," said Sam. This casual attitude between differing levels of employee was endemic and also encouraged. All were on first name terms, regardless of what work they did.

"What have you got for us?"

Sam started talking as he quickly prepped the netbook and projector.

"We all know *Guitar Hero*, right?" he said, for the moment talking with his back to them. He linked up the cable and turned on the projector before turning around. "A decent bit of software with good hardware sales too. Sold millions, had people across the globe interacting with a plastic guitar and thinking they were rock stars."

There were a couple of easy laughs from the managers.

"And then came *Rock Band*, where you plugged a real guitar into the console and actually *did* become a rock star. What a stroke of genius *that* was! Not only is it a great game, it has a serious application in the real world. Well, my idea is going to stand on the shoulders of those particular giants."

Sam started the slideshow. Two enormous words appeared on the screen: CLIT HERO.

The managers stopped laughing.

"Is this a joke, Sam?" asked one.

"No, I'm entirely serious. We all like sex. We all do it. And we all know about foreplay and we're always getting told how bad we are at it." Sam clicked the mouse button and the slide changed to a 3D image of a cut-out section of a woman, from the hips to the top of the thighs, complete with a partially dilated vagina. There were a couple of buttons embossed on the side. It was obviously a mock-up of a new piece of hardware.

"This will come in pink, brown and black, obviously," said Sam.

One of the managers leaned forward. "Seriously?" he asked.

"Absolutely!" said Sam, buzzing with enthusiasm. "This game will do for foreplay what *Rock Band* did for musicians. Players score points as a sensor inside the hardware monitors their cunnilingus skills. They get bonuses for bringing the hardware to 'orgasm'."

"You're actually supposed to lick this thing?" asked one.

"Yep," said Sam. "But there'll be a mode for using fingers as well."

"How do players hold the hardware?" asked another. "Do they pick it up?"

"Like this," said Sam, holding his hands in front of his face about a foot apart. He furiously waggled his tongue in the air.

The managers sat and stared at Sam, and then at the image on the screen, for what seemed like an eternity.

"I like it," said one at last. The others murmured their agreement. By the end of the meeting, there was a general consensus to test the idea in a few focus groups and Sam was tasked with arranging for a hardware prototype to be knocked up on the company's new 3D printer.

The game was officially announced at the *E3* expo the following year, and the industry was abuzz with expectation. The second most asked question at the expo was "When's *'Clit Hero'* coming out?" (the first, obviously, being "What the fuck is going on with *'The Last Guardian'*?) Pre-orders went through the roof. Upon release, *Clit Hero* topped the charts in 14 countries and reviews were uniformly positive. There was lots of media coverage. Philip Schofield demonstrated the game live on This Morning. People couldn't get enough of it.

On a single percentage point of net profits, Sam quickly became a very wealthy individual. He bought himself a cherry red Corvette Stingray but otherwise restrained any spending urges and carried on much the same as before.

It wasn't too long before he set up another pitch meeting and this time all of the managers attended.

"This time," said Sam, addressing the crowd, "we'll be looking at doing *'Cock Hero'*."

There was much raucous approval.

"It was inevitable, really," one of the managers said to another.

A year later, the game was released, this time to uniformly poor reviews and virtually no sales. **COCK HERO FLOPS** ran the headlines. For whatever reason, there was much reluctance on the part of the predominantly male demographic to incorporate fellatio into their skill-sets.

The company lost a *lot* of money. Sam never pitched any more ideas.

WC Blues

It was the old familiar rumble in the guts. Jack had been there a thousand times before. Trapped wind, bloating, the heavy feeling of solids that needed letting go. He fought against the urge to rush to the toilet and let it all out.

Jack had *parcopresis*, a terrible fear of emptying his bowels in a public toilet, especially when other people were also using the restroom. Many people suffer from this awful fear but Jack's phobia was more acute than most and however bad the pain he simply wouldn't give in to the urge.

This had been going on for over a decade. His body would tell him he needed to take a dump and every work day he'd order his body to keep the waste inside himself, to stay in his bowels until he could clock off, tear along the motorway a few junctions and speed back to his house to his own toilet.

How he loved his toilet, his own private little sanctuary where he'd let out a great sigh and a torrent of solids would erupt from his backside, splattering the pan to a chorus of raucous trumps and wheezing noises. Once or twice the waste came out so fast his anus made a whistling sound, which Jack might have found amusing had he not been bent double with the pain of it all.

His body could only take so much of this. With the familiar rumbling bringing tumult to his guts, and with the Deflatines failing to work their magic, Jack squirmed in his chair and got a sweat on. It was not yet ten o'clock and the rest of the office workers were going about their business as usual, unaware of Jack's dilemma. His skin felt cold and clammy and the shirt under his armpits was starting to get wet.

Something inside was trying to force its way out. He had to use all of his focus to tighten his sphincter until not even a loose atom could get through. His guts were in revolution, his ring straining. It felt like his insides were alive, writhing like snakes. This was the worst it had even been. Jack's skin had turned pale and he was covered in a sheen of sweat. When he imagined that the turds inside him had turned around and were making an attempt to come up into his throat he knew that he couldn't hold back any longer and finally, after all these years, he would have to cave in to the urge.

He stood and walked awkwardly out of the office to the restroom area. He noticed that two of the cubicles were already in use but he no longer cared, throwing open the door of the nearest one and pulling down his trousers and pants before flopping down on the pan and letting go.

It exploded out of him like a slurry hose on double pressure, so forcefully he gasped aloud and his backside was splattered with water and shit, accompanied by a noise like a chainsaw cutting down an oak. It seemed to go on forever and he groaned, elated with relief but consumed by the pain as his sphincter stretched itself wide enough to birth this heaving torrent of filth.

A concerned voice spoke up from one of the other cubicles.

"Everything all right in there, mate?"

Jack ignored the voice and concentrated on emptying himself. The pressure had lifted but things were still sliding from his arse, hot and sticky and longer than he would have thought possible. He winced with pain as he felt something inside being pulled.

After a few more seconds, he risked a look, parting his legs and letting his gaze fall on the pan beneath himself.

"Gah!" he cried, seeing the worst.

The pan was full of brown and red, shit and blood, and there were glistening pink things hanging out of him, coiling on top of the mountain of muck. Tentatively, he tried to stand a little and cried again when something tore in his stomach. Long tubes of intestine slipped further into the pan.

He'd prolapsed. All these years of holding back the filth had destroyed his insides and now they were sliding out of him. He sat back down, his mind in turmoil. Offal continued to ooze down into the pan and he wondered what to do. Was he dying? Was this it, an ignomious end in a tiny cubicle in a nondescript office block on a bland trading estate?

The other cubicles had emptied and he was alone. He thought about calling for help but remained quiet. It was too late for help. What could anyone do for him now? If he wanted to get out of this mess he'd have to do it himself.

He took his car keys out of his trouser pocket and reached down to begin sawing away at his intestines. He was light-headed and dizzy but strangely there was no pain any more. He hacked and sawed until most of his guts fell into the pan and only a few loose ends remained. He used his fingers to push these back inside himself.

He stood, swaying. He didn't know how but he was still alive. He pulled his trousers and pants up, not bothering to wipe himself down, and opened the door. His hands were disgustingly filthy, covered in the remains of all sorts of indescribable muck, but he didn't feel like washing them. It didn't matter. Nothing would matter any more.

Jack walked out of the restroom, leaving a single red and brown handprint on the door. He didn't go back to his desk. Instead, he walked out of the building and into the bright sunlight of the day. There was nothing left for him in there.

He left his car in the car park and started walking. A new future dawned, one where his old life didn't matter. The sun was shining and he no longer had a care in the world.

He felt amazing.

Two Magpies

The European magpie *(pica pica)* is one of the most intelligent creatures on the planet, right up there with chimps, dolphins and octopuses. They're not going to enslave humans any time soon but you can be sure they give it some thought every now and then.

Magpies are social creatures, a trait of the *corvidae* family to which they belong. It's probable that their intelligence emerged as a by-product of this sociability. To keep track of attributes of fellow clan members - who is nice, who isn't, who will trade, who is having relations with who and so on - takes a lot of brains.

One thing that magpies enjoy is a bit of roadside dining, particularly when the meal on offer is fresh. A badger had been squashed by an articulated lorry and its innards lay steaming in the road. The dead beast had burst open and the look of shock on its face had lasted less than a minute before another vehicle came along and crushed its skull into flattened mush.

Two magpies had watched the carnage from a nearby tree and, with the machine-gun clatter of raucous celebration, they flew down to the kerb and hopped out into the road for a closer look.

"Some good stuff here, Dave," said one, pecking at a string of badger guts.

"You're not wrong," said Dave, a little tongue flicking out from his beak.

Magpies aren't noted for their sentimentality. There was little thought given to the dead badger and its tragic end.

They pecked bits of glistening offal from the pile in the road, swallowing chunks whole. After a minute or so, Dave called out a warning and they hopped back onto the pavement to let a van drive past. The wind ruffled their feathers and they returned to their meal.

As he threw back his head to try and let a particularly big chunk of something slide down his gullet, Phil's eyes were trained skyward and caught sight of an approaching figure. He swallowed.

"Heads up," he said.

"What is it?"

"Bob's coming."

"Ah, not Bob. Get your fill, that greedy bastard won't leave much."

Bob was larger than his fellows and as he landed next to them his belly wobbled beneath his feathers. He stretched his wings and shook them, scattering a cloud of dust motes.

"All right?" he said, nodding at the others. "Go a bit of badger, have we? Mind if I have a go?"

"Help yourself, Bob," said Dave. They didn't want to share but Bob could get a bit lairy at times and it wasn't worth aggravating him. They kept to the edge as Bob waded right into the guts and buried his head. When he re-emerged his feathers were glistening with gore.

"Mmm," said Bob, swallowing something with his eyes closed. When he opened them again he spotted something further out in the road. "Is that a...?" he said, more to himself than the others. It was, indeed, a sweetbread, something that Dave and Phil had spotted but were too cautious to tackle as it was stuck to the badger's fur and would need a bit of wrestling to extract. With the speed some of the vehicles came along it was too dangerous.

Bob didn't think so. He hopped over and started tugging. Almost as if on cue, a small black car came tearing around the corner and hurtled towards him. Phil cried out a warning (although Dave deliberately remained quiet) but it was too late. Bob was too fat to get out of the way in time. The car didn't even slow down, it slammed into Bob as he flapped to get out of the way and he exploded against the grill before being flung to the side of the road.

Phil and Dave stood staring as the wind from the car finished ruffling their feathers. There wasn't much left of Bob. His head was sort of hanging off and his breast had split open. He looked thinner now that half of his innards were gone. Phil hopped a bit closer.

"Is that a...?" he said.

"I think it might be," said Dave.

"Dibs!" cried Phil. He buried his head in Bob's remains and fished out a little sweetbread. With a quick chobble it slipped down his throat and he let out a little avian belch. "That was lovely, Dave," he said.

They had a bit more badger, until they were full, and then they stretched and flew back to the high branches of a tree to look down on the world. Bob was already a distant memory.

"What do you fancy doing today?" asked Phil.

"Dunno."

"Someone's put a bit of washing out over there. Shall we go and shit on it?"

"In a bit, yeah. That pigeon with the gammy leg needs a good kicking again later."

"OK, but I'll be seeing Mildred at some point."

"I dunno what you see in her," said Dave.

"I think I love her."

"You soft twat."

The latter part of the afternoon was spent torturing a lapwing chick that had become separated from its parents. Phil and Dave took turns in attacking the chick whilst patrolling the immediate area to stop any attempt at rescue. It was a fun game. The object was to stab the chick with their beaks, causing terrible damage, but not to kill it. Whoever made the fatal blow was the loser. If they were hungry they would eat the dead chick but often they would just leave it.

After that, Dave said he wanted a quick bath and Phil should go ahead and wait by the unfortunate pigeon who was lined up for a kicking. Phil waited for a long time. Dave, being a typical magpie completely without sentiment, loyalty or honour, was busy giving Mildred a good seeing to behind Phil's back.

The Joke

Gary Griggs parked and looked around his old stomping grounds. Here, at this university, was where his life really started. Getting away from his miserable home, meeting like-minded new people, finding his wings and learning to fly... And now he was back, as a professional stand-up comedian, to do a benefit gig. The only payment was travel expenses, which he would have ordinarily turned down but with the price of petrol these days...

He walked across campus and headed for the student bar. It was early afternoon, and he'd been summoned by the booker to go over a few things before the gig. Gary didn't mind, it would give him a chance to wander the grounds and soak up the atmosphere. Maybe get a couple of pints in first.

He entered the bar and saw that it was mostly empty. In the gloom, he noticed a young man sitting in the corner. Next to him was a table of four young men and two women playing some sort of board game. The bar music, muted and on low volume, was Ed Sheeran. Gary hated Ed Sheeran.

"Philip?" he called out.

The man glanced up and looked him up and down. "Yes?" he asked.

"Gary Griggs. I'm on tonight."

"I see. Come over here and sit down please."

When he here as a student, Gary used to do Philip's job. Booking bands, comedians and other entertainment. Although now bald, back then he had spiky black hair and wore eyeliner. He spent most of his university life half-cut. They were easily the best years of his life. He once booked the Jim Rose Circus and even though it was thirty years ago he still remembered every part of that act. People skewering themselves. A man drinking a pint of sick. Disgusting but totally hilarious.

Philip hadn't yet smiled or made any friendly overtures.

"Everything alright?" asked Gary.

"I'd just like to risk-assess your material before we do the final sign-off."

"Risk assess? Don't worry, I'm not going to incite a riot."

Philip looked most unimpressed with Gary's response. "Please," he said, "if you don't mind. Can you quickly run through your set?"

"Seriously? Is that what you brought me in for?"

"Of course."

"Can I at least get a pint in?"

"We don't allow our entertainers to consume alcohol before or during the performance."

Gary looked at the little twerp with a sense of rising dread. Things had definitely changed.

"From the beginning?" asked Gary, now focusing so he could get through this ordeal as quickly as possible. He hoped the rest of the students weren't going to be as uptight as Philip or it was going to be a very long night.

"Yes."

"OK. So the act starts out deliberately cliched and old-school. It's a set-up for a routine later in the act. I say hello and then start with a classic 'man walks into a bar' gag."

"You can't do that," said Philip.

"Do what?"

"Tell a joke like that."

"Why not?"

"It's exclusionary."

"Sorry, you've lost me."

"Does it have to be a man?"

"Well, yes. That's what a 'man walks into a bar' joke is all about. It's a cultural touchstone of the comedic landscape. What is your objection?"

Philip looked pained.

"Are you saying it should be a woman?" asked Gary.

"Is there any need to define the gender at all?" countered Philip.

Gary started at him.

"Can you say 'non-binary' person instead?" asked Philip.

"I suppose," said Gary, already thinking that such a subversive approach to a classic gag might work in his favour with the right crowd.

"And you can't have them walking into a bar," added Philip.

"Why not?"

"For one, you're excluding non-bipedals. And we wouldn't want to promote the idea of consuming alcohol."

"But I'll be performing in a bar." Gary waved an arm to take in the room they found themselves in. "This is a fucking bar."

"If you're going to swear then this meeting will be terminated. Final warning."

The people at the next table looked up from their board game. Two of them tutted.

"Are you kidding me?" asked Gary, incredulous.

"The use of swearwords is an intimidating and oppressive action that will not be tolerated."

"You're saying I'm oppressing you right now?"

"I'm finding your manner unnecessarily aggressive, yes."

Gary took a deep breath. Over the last couple of years, people like Philip had exerted growing power over him. He knew comedians that had packed it all in after this overly-sensitive generation had cancelled them on social media over one gag or another. You couldn't make a joke about anything these days, or say something funny without some snowflake fuckwit virtue signalling their small-mindedness by trying to destroy a career that had been years in the making.

At that moment, he saw his entire future crumble to nothing. Universities used to be hotbeds of conflicting opinion. They used to be the nursery of ground-breaking ideas, populated by the coolest kids around. Now they were sterile breeding grounds for identikit, culturally lobotomised idiots. More than anything in the world he wanted to smack this self-imposed Guardian for the Easily Offended on his backside with a stout punch to the nose. He took a deep breath and sighed.

"This non-binary person-"

"Good, yes..." interrupted Philip.

"-walks into a-"

"No, remember we mentioned the bipedal thing..."

"Ok, this non-binary paraplegic-"

"Better, yes..."

"-rolls into a bar-"

"No, not a bar!"

"-rolls into a butcher's shop-"

"No!"

"OK, this non-binary vegan paraplegic rolls into a bakery and asks for a pint – no, wait a minute – asks for a loaf of bread."

"OK, great so far," said Philip.

There was a long pause as Gary tried to think of a way to end this new gag. A bead of sweat broke across his brow. Christ, he couldn't think of anything. And this was only the first joke. He sighed again, and accepted defeat. His career as a comedian was officially over.

"Well?" asked Philip.

"Well, what?" snapped Gary. He could feel the veins in his temple throbbing.

"What's the damned punchline?"

A broken man, his future in tatters, his dreams no more than smoking ashes on a bleak landscape where nothing was allowed to be funny anymore, Gary summoned up enough enthusiasm to give Philip a physical punchline he would long remember. It wasn't the right thing to do, of course, but as he walked out of that bar with a gaggle of stunned faces watching him go – with one filming on a mobile phone and Philip clutching a bloodied nose - he at least felt momentarily fulfilled.

The next day, the clip went viral, Gary was de-platformed and the fight for our culture continued.

Anti-Claus

When December came, everything in the village changed. Once vibrant voices grew hushed and the tinkle of laughter fell away. Joy was forgotten. A blanket of fear descended, heavier even than the prodigious snowfall. People hurried through the streets, afraid to be out alone after dark.

He was coming.

Santa Claus.

Every year it was the same but the burden never got any easier. In the summer months, when the bright sunshine reigned supreme, there was always a little knot of fear in the villagers' stomachs, knowing that the reprieve was only temporary. Winter would soon come, and with it the iron grip of the cold and the infinite darkness.

With two weeks to go, final preparations began. All decorations and ornaments were taken down, boxed up and hidden in attics. The indoor trees, situated in the corners of every village house and nurtured throughout the year, were taken outside and left to fend for themselves until January broke. The favourite toys of all the children were put to one side of the chimneys and left untouched. So too were the items most prized by the adults.

When the time came, in the dark and early hours of the 25th of December, Santa Claus would crawl down their chimneys and take what he wanted.

Lily Tomlinson had been badly-behaved all year – bottom of the class in virtually every subject and always forgetting to do her homework. She'd not once helped her mother with the housework, despite being asked often. Her face was usually scrunched in a scowl and she was always climbing trees and coming home covered in muck. At least once a week she'd be involved in a fight, usually with one of the boys. She was getting a bit of a reputation.

When summer was almost over, her parents had bought her a puppy, in the hope of turning her into a good little girl. Quite how this was to be achieved they had no idea, but they nursed the forlorn hope that the tiny dog would bond with her and somehow bring out an angel that hadn't yet materialised. There could be no doubt that Lily loved that puppy with all her heart, and that the feeling was wholly reciprocated, but having a new, constant companion didn't change her behaviour one bit.

Her parents despaired. They had, in their foolishness, given her the one thing that Santa Claus would certainly take, which would only make the following year even more unbearable.

But there was another fear, lurking in their bellies. Every year, the most badly-behaved of the villagers was lashed to death out on the village green, their skin flayed in great strips as Santa's reindeer-hide whip gouged deep crimson wounds and sent blood flying across the pristine, white snow. The others, even the children, would peer through the gaps in their curtains, cold sweats on their own skin, until the deed was over. Only when Santa Claus was gone would they come out and tend to the body, which would be buried at noon the next day. The name of the deceased would be added to the list of Terrible People, carved into the stone marker at the crossroads.

There could be no greater disgrace.

Her parents hoped that this year, it wouldn't be Lily out there.

On the 25th of December, in the early hours of the morning, a clatter reverberated through the house as something large forced its way down the chimney and into the Tomlinson's lounge. Awake, too frightened to move, Lily's parents cowered under their blanket and listened, their ears straining. They heard Santa Claus rummaging through their belongings, and a short, deep growl of appreciation when he found something he wanted.

And then came the sound of his footsteps on the stairs.

Clump-clump-clump.

Heavy footsteps, a grunt accompanying each one.

In her bedroom, Lily was awakened by growling. Pongo was standing at the end of their bed, his hackles raised, staring and snarling at the door. Lily sat up and listened. Footsteps made their way along the landing.

He was outside.

The bedroom door opened. A bulky figure stood in the doorway, somehow blacker than the darkness around it. The dog let out a small whine and was silent. Lily felt her feet grow warm. Pongo, in his terror, had wet the bed.

Santa Claus stepped into the room. He waited, saying nothing, only the sound of his heavy breathing in the darkness.

"What do you want?" asked Lily, her voice barely more than a croak.

"The dog," said Santa. His voice was deep. Gravelly. Very, very old. "Give it to me."

Lily reached for the dog and pulled it under the duvet.

"Never!" she screamed.

The defiance was only temporary. Santa ripped away the duvet and flung it across the room. With a roar, he grabbed Pongo by the scruff of his neck and, with his other hand, delivered a blow that sent Lily flying from the bed and into the wall. There was a sickening crunch as her neck broke and she lay there, quite dead.

With Pongo whining in terror, Santa clumped his way out of the room and down the stairs. Outside, screams rang through the streets as one of the men-folk was dragged by his hair and tied to the village whipping post by half a dozen small figures dressed in black robes.

"Please!" he wailed. "I haven't done anything wrong!"

"Ho ho ho!" laughed Santa, his deep voice echoing around the village square. "Hasn't done anything wrong! Listen to him!"

With a quick flick of his wrist, he snapped the dog's neck and threw the body into his sack. People were staring through their windows, watching the scene unfold. Some of the braver souls had come out onto the square.

"Let him go!" shouted a woman, but her defiance was fleeting as she fled when Santa turned his gaze on her.

"Listen to me!" he boomed, reaching for his whip. "Thomas Kelp is the worst of all of you, and that is saying something. You people just can't be good, can you? Even though you know I come to punish you, every year without fail, you still think you can get away with whatever you like."

He rolled up his sleeves and tested the whip. The tip broke through the snow and smashed against the cobbled stones, sending a loud *crack!* through the streets.

"What has he done?" asked another voice.

Santa laughed again. "I'll tell you," he roared. "He stole a loaf of bread from his employer. He hit his wife and made her bleed. He lied, just now, about not doing anything wrong. But worse than any of this," he said, turning his gaze on the owner of the enquiring voice before looking down at Thomas Kelp, "he told his only child that I did not exist!"

"I didn't want to scare him," pleaded Kelp, his eyes wide. "I didn't want him growing up in fear like the rest of us."

"QUIET!" shouted Santa. He lifted up his arm and brought the whip down across Thomas Kelp's back. It cut through his shirt and left a ragged tear in the man's flesh. Kelp moaned in terror and pain and Santa brought the whip down again and again until Kelp was silenced.

As the villagers watched, Santa kept whipping until the flesh was lashed from Kelp's bones. The whip came away soaked in blood, flinging great dollops of fatty flesh onto the snow at the villagers' feet. The punishment continued long after Kelp was dead, until the man was no longer recognisable as having once been a living person.

When it was over, Santa held out the whip and it was retrieved by one of his little helpers. He turned to look at the villagers one last time.

"I will see you all again, one year from now," he said, bowing his head. And then he left, walking into the darkness surrounded by his little helpers, off to where they had parked up the sled. In moments, they were flying through the air to the next village.

It was a long night.

Glitter

I've been seeing it for years, ever since I was a boy. Dog shit sprinkled with glitter, out on the streets of my home town. I'd see it so often that I didn't even think it was unusual. Back when it was crumbly white, that's how long ago I'm talking, although you don't see it these days. But shit is always lying around, despite the fines handed out to owners who don't clear up after their pets. Some of them just don't seem to care.

It's not something I pay much attention to, the shit and the glitter, not really. I mean I see it, and sometimes muse on it, but not for long - it isn't something I think about in any great depth. You know that life sometimes has little mysteries that you just accept? Like the way birds sometimes fly into windows, or the way it can rain on one half of the street and not the other? It's like that.

Or rather it was. Because this morning, the mystery was solved. I saw him, this old man, stooping over to pour a little bit of glitter on a fresh turd. It stopped me in my tracks, the craziness of it. And for some reason I needed to know what this was all about. So I followed him.

He did it twice more before he suspected that he was being followed. I'm no sleuth and I wasn't very good at concealing myself. He turned and looked at me for a long time before moving on. At that point I could've walked away but I decided not to. I don't know why. It wasn't really any of my business but now that I'd seen it happening, rather than just seeing the aftermath, my curiosity was piqued. I kept following him, into town, even though this was going to make me late for work.

Eventually he stopped and waited for me to catch up.

"What are you looking at?" he asked.

"Nothing."

"Don't lie. You've been following me. I ain't stupid."

I'd been caught red-handed, there wasn't much point in denying it.

"OK," I said, "you got me. I'm curious, that's all. About the glitter."

"You want me to tell you why I put glitter on the dog shits?"

"Yes."

He looked me up and down and sighed.

"No-one's ever asked before," he said.

"Really? But you must have been doing it for over twenty years."

"More like sixty years, son. Ever since I was a boy." He looked around and pointed at a small café. "Why don't you buy us a hot drink and I'll tell you all about it."

The café was fairly dingy inside. I'd never been there before, never even noticed its existence. We were the only customers. I ordered a tea for the old man and a coffee for myself. The young girl behind the counter (who was very attractive, I noticed) told me to sit and she'd bring them over.

We sat by the window, looking out onto the street. The old man sat quietly, waiting for his drink, occasionally looking my way. He seemed unsure now, as though maybe he thought he'd made a mistake. The drinks arrived and we each took a sip.

"Do you like Christmas, boy?" he asked.

"Yeah. I mean, who doesn't?"

"Not everyone does. If you haven't got any loved ones, or any money, Christmas can be a hard time. The suicide rates go right up at Christmas, did you know that?"

"I think so, yeah."

"It's terrible really. Should be a time for celebration, not for death. You get lots of presents, do you?"

"I used to. Not so much now."

He smiled. "I never used to care much about presents," he said. "My family was dirt poor and I'd be grateful for a fresh orange on Christmas Day. Can you believe that?"

I didn't know what to say. I've never been grateful for a piece of fruit in my life. They're sort of everywhere. I'd have been heartbroken if my parents had fobbed me off with an orange.

"I don't suppose you can," he said, still smiling and looking at me until I had to break eye contact and feign interest in something outside the window. "Youngsters these days get everything they want. It's a different world from the one I grew up in."

I began to wonder where all of this was going. I was conscious of the bollocking I'd get for being late for work – it would be the second time in a week and my boss was only going to take so much. I got the feeling that this old man was a bit lonely and, grateful for company, could sit there talking for hours. As soon as that thought crossed my mind I felt guilty for wanting to get away and deprive him of some human contact.

"I'll tell you about the glitter," he said, as though sensing my thoughts. "Have you ever been to the North Pole?"

"Er, no."

"I have. I loved Christmas so much that I begged my parents to take me. They couldn't afford it, of course. But when some distant relative died and left my father some money, he took me. All those years of thanking him for the oranges must have eaten away at him and this was his was of making amends. We caught a flight up to Lapland on the twenty-second of December and did the whole tourist thing. At least that's what I thought it was – Santa and all his reindeer, all the elves rushing about with toys. Even as a child I knew this was all make-believe. Isn't that right, son?"

"Isn't what right?"

"That it's all make-believe? Some tour company dressing up their employees to make a bit of money from people's stupidity."

"I guess so."

"Wrong!" he said, adding a cackle for good measure. "It's all real! That man I saw really was Santa Claus! They really were elves. And the reindeer, the beautiful reindeer.... They were always my favourites. Rudolph, Dasher, Dancer, Prancer, Vixen, Comet, Cupid, Donner and Blitzen."

"You know all their names from memory?" I asked. "I can never remember more than a couple."

"They were my favourite part of Christmas," he said, his eyes turning misty with nostalgia. "More than the presents, more than the elves, more than Santa, even.... I loved the reindeer and spent most of my time in the

North Pole petting them. They were magnificent beasts. Anyway, as things turned out, there was something wrong with the plane that was supposed to fly us home so we ended up staying another couple of days until they sorted it out. We saw Santa and his reindeer fly off on Christmas Eve to deliver the presents. And we were still there when they came back."

He trailed off and I noticed that his eyes were glazed over. A single tear rolled down his cheek.

"What happened?" I asked.

"The reindeer had aged terribly overnight. They were so exhausted from flying around the world, delivering all those presents, it had taken everything from them. One by one, as I watched in horror, the poor creatures dropped down dead in the snow. My father tried to drag me away but I ran over to Rudolph and flung myself across him. He was still warm. I stayed there until he turned cold.

"That's really sad," I said. And it was. I hadn't really thought about it before but I suppose it was obvious that a reindeer's workload was so strenuous that it could only prove fatal.

"I found out that Santa Claus needs to replace his reindeer every year," he said. "He needs the fittest youngsters he can find – only the healthiest will make it through Christmas Eve, but even the strongest cannot live past Christmas Day. The toll on their bodies... it's too much."

"I'll bet that ruined Christmas for you," I said.

"And you'd be right. But it's not the worst thing."

"There's something worse?"

"What do you think happens to them?" he asked.

"The reindeer? I don't know. Do they get buried?"

"No. They get ground up and used for food."

"Really? Santa's reindeer? What, like reindeer steaks?"

"Not food for humans. They've used so much muscle power through the night that their flesh is too tough for people. Even if you slow-cooked it for three days it'd still be as tough as old leather. Santa chops them up and-"

"Santa?" I blurted, appalled.

"Oh, yes. Didn't you know Santa is a butcher? In the old days, his suit was white, all white. But, over the years, enough people have seen him after he's butchered the reindeer that he couldn't continue with white and changed his outfit to red. To hide all the bloodstains, see. The last thing he wants is for a child to see him covered in blood – imagine how *that* would ruin a child's Christmas."

I took a big slurp of coffee and wrinkled my face. It suddenly tasted so bitter. This was the most horrible story I'd ever heard. Santa – a butcher! Chopping up his reindeer! It couldn't be true. But something in the old man's eyes told me it was.

"So what does eat the reindeer?"

"Dogs. They get chopped up and then Santa loads them into a mincer and bags everything up for export. It all ends up in dog food."

"So why the glitter?" I asked.

"A mark of respect. Every bit of dog shit out there contains a little bit of Santa's reindeer. Putting a bit of glitter on the turds is my way of thanking them for their sacrifice."

He sat there and stared at me for a while before lifting his mug and drinking the rest of his tea.

"Happy now that you know?" he asked.

"Not really."

"Well, you know what they say about curiosity. Thanks for the tea, son. I'll be seeing you."

I watched as he shuffled out of the café and he gave a final nod as he passed by the window. I sat there for a while, my thoughts in turmoil. What a downer. This was going to upset me for days. I slowly stood and walked towards the door and the girl behind the counter thanked me for my custom.

I gave her a sad smile. She really was beautiful. I suddenly thought of a way to make the world a happier place, for me at least. Without stopping to consider the possibility that she might turn me down, I opened my mouth and asked her if she'd like to go for a drink somewhere, after she'd finished for the day.

"I'm sorry, I have a boyfriend," she said, looking a little sorry for me. I smiled, nodded, and left the café. It took a few minutes to walk to work and, when I arrived, my boss shouted at me that I'd been late one time too many and sacked me on the spot.

What a horrible day. I didn't think it could get any worse but on the long walk home I stepped in a huge pile of dog shit. I looked down at the horrible brown mess covering the sole of my shoe and noticed that there wasn't even any glitter in it.

BONUS
SHORT
STORY

The Pike

The Pike

Yap yap yap.

Yap yap yap yap yap yap yap yap.

All day, all night, that's what I heard coming through the walls. It kept me awake in the early hours, gritting my teeth in bed and trying to avoid thoughts of kicking down the neighbour's front door and going on a murderous rampage. It got so bad I couldn't think straight any more. Christine – that's my wife – thinks I dwell on it too much, that I should 'live and let live'. Christine, you see, sleeps like a dead thing. I doubted she'd wake up if a nuclear bomb went off, so a few yips from a Chihuahua hasn't exactly bothered her.

It hasn't deepened the worry lines around her eyes the way it has mine.

I'd asked the neighbour – Mrs Tomlinson – to do something about it but she just fake-smiled a mostly toothless grin and told me to "Piss off!" She's a charmer. I can't believe she's made it past eighty without anyone killing her. She's as deaf as a post, so the yapping doesn't bother her either.

It only bothers me. It seems to be my problem alone.

When she moved in, about ten years ago, we thought it might be nice to have a sweet old lady living next door. Christine even baked her a cake as a welcome gift. Christine's not a great baker so maybe that's what did it, or maybe Mrs Tomlinson was already a cantankerous old git when she arrived and the cake made no difference at all. For all we knew, she could have been that way all her life (and that's pretty much what I've concluded).

Whatever it was, any inchoate feelings of friendliness quickly dissipated and we'd only spoken to each other since when any kind of neighbourly dispute came up.

Our garden fence blew down in a gale one night and we got a new one, which, on many occasions, she let us know that she hated. It was the wrong colour, and after we Creosoted it the colour was still not to her liking. She complained to the council about us having overfilled waste bins a few times – once when the bloody bin men were on strike! She even complained when we had a family barbeque one Summer afternoon, standing looking over the new fence and shouting whilst our entire family looked at her angry little face as it sprayed spittle all over the lawn. But all of this paled to insignificance in comparison to the sleepless nights I endured because of that fucking dog.

She had the Chihuahua when she came. Such a pair were never better suited. It was a manky little ball of hate. It even looked the same as her, with little tufts of white hair poking out of the top of its head, the bulging eyes and a mouth mostly empty of teeth. It had enough to draw blood though, that much I knew from direct experience. First time I ever saw it, way back when we were still talking to the old bag, I said *"Aah!"* and reached down to give it a bit of fuss and the thing gave a screech and leapt at my hand, sinking its gnarly teeth into my finger. It took over a minute for the little bastard to let go, and a minute's a long time in a situation like that.

When we got our own dog, about four years ago, we made sure it wasn't a Chihuahua – anything but a little yappy thing because a stereophonic yap would had sent me over the edge completely. We got ourselves a Highland terrier and he's everything you could ever want in a dog. Jack is friendly, always pleased to see you, never shits in the house, chews only the things he's supposed to and hardly ever barks, even when next door's little monster is going at it full tilt.

I called the Environmental Health people from the council and they sent a guy round with some recording equipment. The Chihuahua barked on cue but the man said that although it was an irritant, it wasn't loud enough to be a nuisance.

"You say that when you haven't had a decent night's sleep in ten years," I told him but he smiled apologetically and said that there wasn't much he could do. I couldn't believe this and must have spent twenty minutes trying to convince him otherwise. Finally, in an act of desperation, I asked him what he would do if he were me and the council refused to help.

"Dunno. Get an air rifle?"

I thought about it, I really did. I'm normally horrified at the thought of cruelty of any kind to an animal (with the exception of maggots, which will become clear) but this dog had been driving me to distraction and I was at the end of my tether. I could have shot it from the bedroom window whilst it was in old Tomlinson's back garden and even though it would have been obvious what had happened, I thought as long as I dumped the air rifle immediately afterwards no-one would ever be able to prove it was me. I mean, nobody would seriously investigate the matter to the point of ordering ballistics reports or anything. Mrs Tomlinson might suspect it was me but what could she do about it?

I thought it best to run the idea past Christine. She was appalled that I could even think such a thing was worth considering.

"Have you heard yourself?" she said, looking at me like I was insane. "Shooting a poor little dog? Is this the man I married?"

Of course, I didn't do it. Christine was right. I couldn't bring myself to shoot that odious creature, I just couldn't. Many mornings since, when I'd lain awake since the early hours – *yap yap yap!* – I'd bitterly regretted my decision.

Luckily, I had something that I relied on to calm me down a bit – fishing. That was my Zen space, a few hours a week when I could blot everything else out of my mind and just completely relax. I was a middle-aged man with a healthy disposable income so it goes without saying that I had all of the gear. (So much gear, in fact, that it was starting to do my head in and these days I seemed to leave a lot of it back at home.) I'd discovered I was happy enough with just a rod, a folding chair, a tub of writhing maggots, a couple of lagers and a good book. Quite often that's how you'd find me, sat on the edge of the pool in the old quarry, reading or dozing and generally being as still and as quiet as it's possible to be in today's world.

It wasn't even about the fishing. Of course, it was always a thrill to actually catch one, but it was never a measure of success and even when I did get a bite the feeling of euphoria was short-lived and I'd unhook the little blighter and pop it back in the pool. In my day I'd caught many trout, grayling, tench, roach, bream, a few minnows and the odd eel. It didn't matter much to me what fetched up on the end of the line, a catch was a catch – I never got excited about the size of the fish, as many other anglers do. For me, fishing was more about just finding the time to spend in my own company, away from other people and, even though I love her dearly, that includes my wife. The act of fishing was just an excuse, really, a way to disguise a few hours of genuine idleness.

And it was a way of spending some time in quiet, often beautiful places I'd never otherwise see. Admittedly the quarry couldn't immediately be appreciated as beautiful but, in its own way, it really was. Rock had been chopped out of the landscape here for over a century and that only stopped about twenty years ago, in which time nature had done everything it could to try and reclaim the land for itself. The hardiest of plants, mostly weeds, had split rock after seeding in the most unlikely spots and although weeds have a bad reputation many of them can be quite colourful and pleasing to look at. When it rained, the rock glistened and, if you went looking, you could sometimes find fossils and imprints from creatures that once walked in these very spots some 60 million years ago.

We lived at the edge of town so all this was just five minutes from the house. I could walk there easily enough but always drove to save lugging my equipment by hand.

The pool itself was magnificent. About seventy metres in diameter, the body of water filled a pit whose depths nobody quite knew. The water was so clear – so crystal clear – that you could easily see to a depth of about twenty metres before a blue tinge quickly darkened to an impenetrable blackness. You could see the fish swimming around as clear as you could see the birds in the sky. Lately, there were so many fish it was almost impossible not to catch one or two every visit. Most times I'd been I'd had the place to myself and it's hard to think of a more pleasing spot I'd rather be on a Saturday morning.

Christine had a habit of asking me if I was going fishing even though she always knew the answer would be yes.

"You off fishing today then?" she'd asked this morning.

"Yep."

"Want me to make up a flask?"

"Please."

"Sandwich?"

"That would be lovely, thanks."

It was pretty much the same conversation, *verbatim*, every weekend. I didn't mind, it was just one of those funny little routines that happily married couples have. She didn't have to ask and, come mid-morning, I always appreciated a flask of hot tea and a cheese sandwich.

"Are you going to drop those record's over to Dad's afterwards?"

Gah. For the last couple of weeks I'd been promising to drop off a load of old vinyl at her parents' house but just hadn't gotten around to it. A large plastic crate filled up most of the boot in my car. They only lived a 15 minute drive away but I just hadn't found the right moment. They were her father's old LP's and 78's, mostly ancient crooners, and had been temporarily stored in our loft when they moved to a bungalow. That was three years ago. The way I saw it, it wasn't exactly urgent.

"I might do," I said. "We'll see how it goes."

"You're bloody hopeless.

As Christine walked from the kitchen, her right foot skidded on the tiled floor and she let out a gasp whilst simultaneously reaching for the door frame to steady herself. My reaction times were much slower these days – had she fallen there's no way I would've been able to stop it.

"I thought I told you to take those shoes back," I said, frowning.

"It's not the shoes."

"Of course it is. You don't go slipping and sliding in any other footwear."

"But I like them."

"That's not the point."

"It must have been something wet on the floor," she said, making a show of examining the tiles but we both knew it wasn't.

On the kitchen counter, my mobile phone started to ring. Graham, my younger brother was calling.

"All right?" I said.

"Not bad."

"What's up?"

"Need a favour."

"How much?"

We'd never been big on small talk. Whenever Graham needed a favour it was usually to borrow some money. He'd had a tough time of it lately. As a graphic designer, he'd worked for two magazine publishing companies that had both folded in the last few years and now he was freelancing he struggled to land the contracts. He was brilliant at what he did but wasn't so hot at selling himself and getting work from new clients. He'd borrowed a bit here and there from me and always paid me back when he came into some money.

"Four hundred."

"OK, no problem."

"Don't you want to know what it's for?"

"It doesn't matter, I know you'll pay me back."

"It's for the car. I have an oil leak and need a couple of tyres. Possibly the brakes need doing too."

"I said you don't have to tell me what it's for."

"Yeah, I know, but I don't want you to think I'm spending it on drugs and hookers."

Graham would be the last person I'd expect to blow money on drugs and hookers. He was a real homebody, loved nothing more than sitting down to a good box-set on Netflix and cooking himself a nice meal. Like most things he put his mind to he was very good at cooking – were he not a graphic designer he could easily have been a chef. It's just a pity he has no-one to cook for apart from himself. Sometimes, when we invite him over, he offers to cook for us. We usually take him up on it. The man can work magic with a handful of ingredients and a few spices.

"Sounds more interesting than spending it on the car," I said.

There was a silence for a second or two and then he changed tack.

"I got a new job," he said.

"Well done. Who with?"

"Some advertising agency based in Ludlow."

"Where the fuck's Ludlow?"

"About sixty miles away, that's why I need the car in good shape. It's a staff job. Not a contract."

"That's great! So you're an employee again? Is the money good?"

"It's pretty shit but it'll be regular. I have to learn a load of new stuff. They do a lot of online and social media campaigns. Can you transfer that dosh into my bank this morning?"

"Yeah, I'll do it before I head off."

"Fishing?"

"What else? When do you start the new job?"

"Monday, that's why the car thing is a rush. Listen – thanks, ok?"

"No worries. Good luck for Monday. I'll transfer that money in the next 5 minutes."

"Thanks, Mickey." Of everyone I knew, he was the only one to call me that, had done ever since we were kids.

"Text me Monday night, let me know how you get on."

"Will do."

We hung up at the same time and then I did a bank app BACS transfer to his account. Half an hour later I was fishing.

I could tell immediately that something was a little off. There was a black Land Rover in the scraggy bit of land used as a car park when I arrived and when I walked through with my gear a man in a green jacket and a flat cap was standing at the edge of the pool and peering into the water. He turned and looked at me as I set up my chair and rod and then walked over.

"Spot of fishing?" he asked.

What a question.

"Yes," I said. "I come here most Saturdays."

"Do you now?" he asked, looking me up and down. "Have you asked the landowner if fishing is allowed?"

"I have no idea who the landowner is," I said. "Nobody knows."

"Well, it's me."

"Oh. Right. So... is it all right if I fish here?"

"Of course it is," he said breaking into a broad smile and extending his hand. "Name's Jim."

"Mike."

"Pleased to meet you, Mike."

"So, you own this place?"

"Have done for about 20 years, ever since they stopped quarrying here and the land became useless overnight."

"It's a lovely spot."

"It is, isn't it? I think that's why I bought it. I could see the potential. Anyone else would've had a shopping centre or a block of flats here by now but I've just let it go to pasture, so to speak."

"Are they your fish?" I asked, nodding towards the pool.

"They are. Every now and then I tip a load of small ones in but I haven't done that for a while. In fact, they've been doing rather well here, so much so that I've had to take measures to curb them a little."

That sounded ominous.

"Curb them?" I asked, prompting him to continue.

"Follow me," he said, walking towards the edge of the pool. I did, and we stood side by side looking into the water. The fish were really active today, darting about all over the place.

"What am I looking at?" I asked.

"Wait for it. You'll see."

We waited. A silence enveloped us, broken only by the buzz of a passing fly. A cloud briefly obscured the sun casting a temporary shadow across the pool.

And then I saw it.

A large fish was gliding through the deep waters, sending everything else scattering before it. It must have been three or four feet long at least, three times the size of any other fish in there. It turned and swam the other way, calm and authoritative. This pool was now his.

"What is that?" I asked. "Is it a pike?"

"Correct," he said. "A proper nasty bastard, if you'll excuse my French. I've had it years."

"How did it get in there?"

"I put it in."

"You did? Why?"

"To curb the numbers. If there are too many fish here it will start attracting the attention of more anglers. I don't mind the odd one but I wouldn't want this place over-run. No offence, mind."

"None taken. Won't it eat all the others?"

"It'll have a good go. It'll probably be a few pounds heavier by the time I take it out."

"And then what will you do with it?" I asked.

"I move it around my fisheries, keep all the other fish on their toes, so to speak."

"How do you catch it? With a rod?"

"With a big net and a pound of raw steak."

"Jesus."

"He likes being caught, by me at least. He knows how well I look after him."

"Him?"

"He's more like a pet. I shouldn't really admit it but I am rather fond of him."

"So, you have other places? Like this?" I asked, my eyes on the dark shape cutting through the water.

"No, nothing like this. This is more like a hobby, an experimentation pond. I sometimes try different groups of fish together to see how they get on."

We watched the pike for a few minutes in silent contemplation and then he turned to me and extended his hand once more.

"I must be off," he said, shaking my hand. "Nice meeting you."

"You too," I said, watching him go. He seemed pleasant enough and it was nice of him to let me stay. I returned to my spot and sat down on my folding chair. I was hungry already and demolished the sandwich whilst sipping hot tea and staring into the pool. Things were getting a little more frantic. The pike had increased its speed and seemed to be actively hunting. The other fish were zooming about all over the place. Underneath the calm surface the pool was in turmoil. As I leaned forward to watch, the pike started honing in on one particular fish and I found myself rooting for it to get away. Wherever it went, the pike was on its tail, getting closer by the second. It was almost too much to watch. Suddenly, the prey changed direction and started swimming furiously up towards the surface – towards *me* – and like something out of a 3D movie it broke the skin of water and launched itself into the air, landing in a flopping mess right at my feet.

I jumped up in alarm, spilling hot tea down my front as I did so. I danced around for a few moments, pulling my shirt away from my chest so I didn't get scalded, flapping the material around to get some cool air circulating. I must have looked like a maniac. When I stopped, I could see the fish – a sizeable brown trout – struggling to breathe.

I didn't know what to do. I looked at the pool and felt the blood freeze in my veins – the pike was there, hanging in the water, looking right at me. The evil bastard was giving me the eye. I could imagine what it was thinking: *Chuck that fish back in here or I'll come right out and get both of you.* It was a terrifying, if ludicrous prospect.

I turned my attention back to the trout. It was dying and didn't have long. There was no way I was throwing it back into the pool, offering it up for sacrifice to that monster. If you'd asked me earlier that morning if I had it in me to feel sorry for a fish I'd have laughed you out of my house but now? I did, I really did.

I ran back to the car and opened up the boot. All those vinyl records went onto the back seat and I ran back with the empty plastic crate. I moved along the pool a little bit and dipped the crate into the water to fill it. The pike moved closer to see what I was up to. I heaved the crate out and walked awkwardly back to my chair. Water is heavier than you'd think and I was knackered after just a few short steps. I put it onto the ground, picked up the trout and gently placed it in. For a few moments I thought it might be dead but it started moving and was soon swimming in a very tight circle.

With a look of disgust, the pike finally turned its attention away from me and resumed the hunt. There was nothing I could do for the others but this little fellow was safe.

But now what? What the hell was I going to do with a trout in a crate full of water? I had no idea, at least for about a minute until I had an extremely stupid idea. I'd take it home with me. It could live in the bath, until I worked out a better solution.

I backed the car up as close as possible and then heaved the crate into the boot before returning to collect my things. Before I set off, I tossed a few maggots in.

"You've done WHAT?!"

It's fair to say that Christine wasn't a fan of the idea. Like I said before, my idea of finding some me-space in the modern world was to go fishing for a few hours. Christine's thing was a nice long soak in the bath, preferably with a glass of wine. She stood in the bathroom doorway looking down at the trout and for a moment I thought she was going to have a heart attack. Her face was bright red. Jack was at her feet, circling and sniffing at the air.

"Calm down!" I urged, squeezing past her. "It's only for the time being."

"I wanted a bloody bath tonight!"

"You can still have one."

"With a fish? Are you mad?"

"I can put it back in the crate until you've finished."

She looked at me in disgust.

"The bath will be all slimy."

"Of course it won't. Fish aren't slimy. Okay, one or two breeds can be but this one isn't."

"Get rid of it."

I hated it when she was like this. Being married for so long, I'd seen this mood hundreds of times and it could last for days. One time I bought a motorbike and she gave me grief non-stop, telling me I was an idiot and that I was going to end up killing myself before my midlife crisis was even over. She shouted that I'd come a cropper and fall off it and she'd be left to grow old with only the dog for company. I had to spend days assuring her that it was perfectly safe and that she was being unreasonable. Of course, the very first time I took it out the bloody thing slid out from under me on a rain-soaked corner and I broke my arm. I sold it for half the price I'd paid for it, spent six weeks in a cast and neither of us mentioned it again.

"I will, but only when I have somewhere for it to go."

"What about that pool where you go fishing?"

"Where do you think I got it from?"

"Well, take it back!"

"I already said, I can't!"

"Why not? It's a bloody pool! There's no better place for it!"

I glanced down at the fish and it seemed to be looking up at me apologetically, as though it felt guilty of causing all the commotion. I wanted to bend over the bath and say a few reassuring words but Christine would've brained me.

"The guy that owns the place has put a pike in there and it'll eat him if I put him back."

"Him?"

Jesus, now *I* was referring to a fish as a *'him'*.

"It."

"Isn't that what fish do? Eat each other?"

"Yes, but..."

"But what?"

"I just can't. It's a *monster*. You should have seen it."

Christine waved her arms in exasperation and stormed off, followed by Jack, telling me to get the fish out and wipe the bath down so she could use it later. I'd left the empty crate in the bathroom so grabbed it and eased it into the bath, gently scooping up the trout with a load of water. I carried it to the spare room and put a few more maggots in. The trout pursed its lips at the surface of the water and nibbled them down.

"It's all right, mate," I said, crouching over the crate. "We'll sort something out for you."

It turned in a tight circle and looked up at me. I tell you, there's not much expression in a fish's face but I could see the gratitude on his – he knew that I'd saved him from that bastard pike and I'm pretty sure he appreciated my current dilemma with Christine. Fish are smarter than you'd think. That old joke about a goldfish having only a few seconds of memory may just be true but once you start getting bigger breeds their brain size increases too. I'm not saying a fish is ever going to quantify String Theory or anything but they aren't the brainless automatons many people think they are. Dolphins were trained during the Second World War to lay mines out amongst the Japanese fleets. Octopuses are now being considered as one of the most intelligent life forms on Earth, after humans and chimps. Not exactly fish, so bad examples, but you get my point.

Christine had her bath and when she was finished I thoroughly cleaned it with cold water so there would be no trace of soap and then filled it up. The trout was gently tipped back in and he swam a few circuits of the tub before looking up at me and, I swear, *smiling*. I was really starting to like this fellow. I wondered if I'd be able to talk Christine into having a large fish tank installed in the lounge.

I kept checking up on him during the evening, just to make sure he was OK. Christine rolled her eyes and sighed but I think she was secretly pleased to have a husband with a caring nature, even if it was being misplaced on a fish. She might have hated it now but I knew, in time, she'd grow to tolerate it. Sometimes I knew my wife better than she knew herself. We owned a cat once, a miserable old bastard we got from a rescue shelter and it caused mayhem for the year or so it was with us. It pissed all over the settee, tore up the curtains, scratched the hell out of both of us and once shat in Christine's jewellery box (*I'd told her not to leave it open!*). That cat made our lives a misery and she often complained how much she hated it but, when it keeled over one day and died of old age, Christine was inconsolable. She cried for three days straight. Its ashes are still on our mantelpiece, in a pewter urn.

We had a quiet evening, with the exception of the usual yapping from next door and a telephone call just after seven. Christine's boss wanted her to deliver some training on Monday afternoon – the original trainer had come down with something and Christine was the only one he felt was up to the job. He actually said that, knowing that the flattery would win her over. She agreed, and then he told her the job was eighty miles away at another office. After hanging up, she spent ten minutes moaning at me about how the traffic was going to be terrible and that she'd probably be late back on Monday so I'd have to get my own dinner sorted. I didn't mind so much, it had been ages since I'd had a Chinese.

Sunday was a quiet affair. I left Christine in bed and nipped out to buy a length of garden hose and a children's paddling pool. By half ten I was back, inflating the pool and then filling it with water from the kitchen tap with the hose. I took Christine breakfast in bed and, whilst she was eating it, carried the trout downstairs in the crate and gently tipped him into the pool, which was a good deal larger than the bathtub.

He raced round and round it, looking at me every now and then to share his joy. He loved it! I'd never seen a happier fish. I felt so glorious I could burst. This must be what having children is like. I fetched a couple of folding chairs from the garage and plonked them next to the pool. The sun was climbing high in the sky and there was a thin layer of wispy cloud that took the edge off the heat. I'd cut the lawn the week before so the threat of that job wasn't looming over me. At that moment, life was about as perfect as it could get.

Christine wandered out into the garden in her dressing gown, looked at the pool and the chairs next to it and then looked back at me. Jack trotted past her and sniffed at the pool. He could tell something was in there.

"Leave it, Jack," I said in a firm voice. He looked up at me inquisitively and then sniffed at the grass before wandering off to do his business.

"Would you like a cup of tea?" she asked.

You see, progress already! No moaning, no rolling of the eyes, not even a sarcastic joke of any kind. She'd looked over the new setup and it was being quietly accepted.

"Yes, please," I said, offering her a warm smile. "You see," I said to Gilbert after she'd gone back inside – *I don't know why but that name just seemed to pop into my head at that moment* – "you're part of the family already!"

He did a little lap of excitement to celebrate.

It was one of those lazy Sunday mornings, where time slowly – and, paradoxically, all too quickly – drifted by. We were in our own little bubble. Nothing else in the world mattered. Christine got up to fetch a cold drink once or twice and otherwise remained engrossed in a book, Jack curled up on her lap. I was happy enough just looking at the pool and letting my mind wander. I pictured us getting a more permanent sort of pool in the garden, which would be a far better idea than having a big glass tank inside the house. Gilbert wouldn't mind the transition outdoors, truth be told he was more of an outdoors fellow anyway. I could dig a big hole in the garden and make a proper rock pool. It would be a centrepiece and Gilbert would be its crown jewel. When friends came over they would marvel at my creation and when they asked where the fish came from I would tell them of my heroism, facing down that evil pike and rescuing Gilbert from certain doom.

I was cruelly brought out of my idle daydreams by the sound of next door's dog barking.

Yap yap yap. Yap yap yap yap yap.

Christine could see me getting agitated.

"Leave it," she warned.

"I'm sick of it."

"Just leave it."

Gilbert had stopped swimming around the pool and was listening in alarm.

"It needs to shut up. It's scaring Gilbert."

"Who the hell is – no. Please tell me you haven't named the fish."

"What's wrong with that?"

"You need help. I'm seriously worried."

Yap yap yap yap yap yap yap.

"I'm going to have to have a word."

"Mike, please. Just let it go."

"But it's wrecking our Sunday."

"*You're* wrecking our Sunday."

"*Me*? What the hell have I done?"

"For God's sake!" Jack sprang from her lap with a little bark and ran around excitedly. Christine dumped her book on the floor, got up and stormed inside the house, followed by the dog and leaving me to contemplate the mysteries of the female species yet again. I sat there trying to work out how I was suddenly the bad guy in all of this and, no matter how I turned the last few minutes over in my mind, I came up with nothing but bafflement. I'd been with Christine for over twenty years, would no doubt be with her until I died and I feared I'd never really understand her.

There was no way I could sit there with all that noise. As soon as I thought that, I realised that it had gone quiet next door. Maybe the dog had gone back inside. I waited, glancing down at Gilbert to see him looking up at me, also waiting. A minute passed. Two. It was still quiet. I dared to lean back in my chair and relax.

I must have drifted off to sleep because the next thing I knew Christine was screaming and all hell was breaking loose.

We'd had no idea that right at the bottom end of the garden, behind the shed, rats had been gnawing away at the fence for months (probably years) and had been making a hole big enough to crawl through. It must have been discovered by the Chihuahua and made even bigger. How it did this with hardly any gnashers is a mystery, but it had just enough teeth to complete the job and force its way through into our garden, where it immediately ran to the inflatable paddling pool and bit a hole in that as well.

The water started trickling, then pouring out, and the pool was quickly on the verge of collapse. The Chihuahua started yapping and Christine came out of the kitchen with two mugs of tea, tripped over the hose I'd forgotten to put away, and screamed as the tea went everywhere. Jack barked and ran after the intruder, trying to play.

I woke with a start.

"What the fuck?" I yelled, taking the scene in. "Gilbert!"

The Chihuahua was yap-yap-yapping, running around my feet and trying to take a bite at my ankles, with Jack close behind it in an attempt to get it to engage in some canine play. I almost tripped over the bloody things as I ran to get the empty crate to rescue Gilbert. Christine was running around flapping her arms at the dogs, trying to shoo away the Chihuahua but it was getting even more excitable amongst all the commotion and then, to add a final layer of mayhem to the proceedings, Mrs Tomlinson poked her manky little head over the top of the fence and started shouting at me.

"What are you doing to my dog, you bleedin' idiot?"

From peaceful silence to utter carnage in sixty seconds.

At the sound of her voice, the Chihuahua raced off back to the hole in the fence and in seconds we heard it yapping away next door. Jack had gone after it so I let Christine deal with that situation whilst I raced Gilbert upstairs to the safety of his bathtub.

"I'm really sorry about all of that," I told him once he was back in. He looked a little out of sorts, as though all of this mayhem had been a bit too much. "You settle yourself down and everything will be all right before we know it." He looked at me, unconvinced.

I went back downstairs. Christine had retrieved Jack, who had managed to get his head through the hole in the fence but not much else. I gave him a little tickle on the chin and then sat down at the kitchen table.

"I'm going to have to do something about that dog," I said.

"Look, it's all over with now so let's just forget about it."

"The shock could have killed Gilbert!" I said and knew immediately that I shouldn't. I knew that such an admission would distract her attention from the real issue at hand and that we'd get into a heated discussion about my affections for our new family member. I think Christine knew how this would play out as well, if we let it. Both of us waited in silence, playing an imaginary escalating argument out in our heads. Sometimes, when you know someone really well, you don't have to go through the bother of doing the real thing, it can be done within the confines of your own head. Thankfully, Christine didn't go down the route of verbalising things.

"Well, there's nothing you can do," she said at last. "You've tried calling it in as a noise pollutant and it didn't work."

"I could put a bit of poisoned meat down?" I suggested, immediately regretting that sentence as well.

"Really?" she asked, in a tone loaded with disgust. "Apart from that being one of the most despicable things you've ever uttered, what if Jack ate it instead?"

"I'd be careful."

"You can't go around poisoning people's dogs, Mike, however annoying they are."

"Don't you want to see it gone?"

"Not as much as you. obviously. Give it a couple of years and the thing will die of old age."

"Are we still talking about the dog? Or old Tomlinson?"

She smiled and flicked the switch on the kettle. I sat there stewing as she made the drinks. There was no way I could let this go, something had to be done. And then I had the idea.

Mrs Tomlinson opened her front door and eyed me suspiciously.

"What do you want?" she asked.

I help up a bottle of port. We knew she liked that stuff and there'd been one in the back of our drinks cabinet for years. If she hadn't been such a cantankerous old witch, she could have had it as a Christmas present a long time ago.

"Can I come in for a chat?"

"What?"

"Can I come in for a chat?"

"You'll have to wait a minute," she said, fumbling around with the controls of her hearing aid. After she was finished she looked at me again, with a dash of added contempt.

"I said 'Can I come in for a chat?'"

Her eyes flitted between me and the bottle. It could have gone either way. Finally, with an exasperated sigh, she opened the door and let me inside. The Chihuahua immediately started trying to bite my ankles and I asked Mrs Tomlinson if she'd mind putting it in another room for a little while. She obliged without saying anything. She must have really wanted to get her hands on that port. With the dog yapping in another room, we sat in her lounge. I handed her the bottle and she placed it onto a table without offering to open it.

"What do you want?" she asked again.

"I want to be a better neighbour," I said, trying not to choke on my own words. "And that begins with an apology for this morning's little episode."

She eyed me for a second or two, her expression giving nothing away.

"You should get that fence fixed," she said. "It's dangerous. My Charlie could have been attacked by your dog, vicious little thing."

I mentally took a deep breath and smiled. One pillar of civilised society is that you can't go around punching old ladies, however vile, just because they said something you didn't like or agree with. There was no doubt that she was a horrible woman but I didn't know the history of her life or why she'd turned out that way. She could have had a terribly difficult life, been beaten down by fate until only a shrivelled lump of hate remained. Then again, she might be an old witch simply because she got pleasure out of it. It wasn't my place to judge.

"Of course," I said. "I'll get onto it this afternoon. Is your dog OK?"

"He's fine, no thanks to you lot."

"I'm glad to hear it."

"Apology accepted. Anything else?"

"Well," I said, leaning forward a little to emphasise what I wanted to say next. "Christine and I were thinking that maybe your little Charlie barks a lot and does things like coming into our garden because he doesn't get out enough."

"He has the back yard to run around in."

"Yes, but does he actually get taken for a walk?"

"What business is that of yours?" She looked angry that I would ask about this.

"Listen," I said, forcing a smile. "I'm only trying to help. I know a lovely little place, only five minutes down the road. It's an old quarry and it's perfect for taking the dog. I know Charlie's old, and walking too far might be a stretch, but do you know what the best exercise is for a dog like Charlie?"

"What's that, then?" she asked. Her voice sounded suspicious but I could tell there was a minute thawing in her demeanour.

"A bit of a swim!" I exclaimed, holding my arms out as if this was the greatest idea the world had ever seen. "Think how Charlie would love a little swim! There's a pool in the quarry, you could stand by the edge and let Charlie have a bit of a dip. A swim would exercise all of his joints and muscles and would be far easier on him than a long walk. It's what all dogs would love – he'd really thank you for it."

"He does get a bit restless in the evenings..." she said.

"Then this is perfect."

"Ah, I'm not sure."

"Think about Charlie. What would he say?"

"He'd probably hate it."

"But you won't know until you've tried it. It could be the best thing he's ever done!"

"We'll have to see..."

"I read somewhere that the benefits of swimming include an increase in life expectancy and less chance of joint pains in old age."

"Is that true?" she asked.

"Absolutely," I said. It must be, right?

"We'll have a think about it."

"I'll pop a map of where the quarry is over your fence later."

I stood up to leave. There was a softening in her expression towards me and I tried not to feel guilty. I hoped I'd been convincing enough to get her to take that dog of hers over to the quarry for a swim, even if it was only the one time.

That pike wouldn't need more than one visit.

I dropped the map across to Mrs Tomlinson later that day (when I knew Christine wasn't looking) and prepared for the fallout, whenever that may come. I'd told Christine that I'd reasoned with the old bat and she'd agreed to take the dog out for a walk more often and left it at that.

We had an early night, interrupted by a spate of yapping at about four o'clock, and then we were both up and out early for work. Neither of us had any idea what a horrible day this would turn out to be. Christine left first, heading for her office to do some prep work before heading out again to deliver her training. After she'd gone, I paid a visit to Gilbert to tell him we'd be gone most of the day but not to worry. I told him I'd pop into the pet shop on my way home to get him some proper food – he loved the maggots but it was a bit of a boring diet. With a last look at him, I closed the bathroom door behind myself and went downstairs.

I left Jack on his bed chewing a treat and drove off to my own job.

When I was a child I thought I was going to be an astronaut when I grew up. Then perhaps a fireman. I suppose most kids – boys anyway – say the same things. What actually happens is that we all grow up and end up in jobs that we hate, stuck in an endless spin-cycle of trying to earn more money for better upgrades on the car, the house, the goddamned mobile phone. I'd been through a fair number of jobs and redundancies, and though I'd hated a lot of them I hadn't done too badly. My current job was based in an office a half-hour's drive from the house. I had my own desk, could get a parking space when I needed one, and there was free coffee. My colleagues were all reasonably nice and I think my boss liked me. For a middle-aged man whose dreams had long since turned to dust, it wasn't that bad a deal. It wasn't too taxing, I wasn't terrible at it and the pay kept us afloat. There was a bit left over for saving towards a good holiday every year.

The work was fairly mundane, a lot of admin and looking at invoices and receipts, the occasional mailshot. During the afternoon, I was in the middle of printing a load of address labels when my mobile rang with a number I didn't recognise. I never get calls on my mobile unless it's from Graham or Christine. I'm not sure why I decided to answer it, I guess I knew that something would be wrong.

"Hello?" I said.

"Is that Mike West?"

"Yes. Who's this?"

"Peter Wilmott. I work with your wife, Christine."

My heart skipped a beat.

“Is something wrong?” I asked, panic rising in my chest.

“It’s nothing to worry about, just a precaution. She’s had a bit of a tumble and banged her head. She’s been taken to the hospital for a check-up, we think she’s got mild concussion. Can you come over? We think you’ll have to drive her home when she’s been seen.”

I quickly wrote down the details of the hospital and looked around the office for my boss.

I’d warned Christine about those bloody shoes!

En route to the hospital I called Graham.

“I need a favour,” I told him. “Christine’s had an accident and she’s been taken to the hospital.”

“Oh, God, no. Is she OK?”

“I think so, she’s had a bit of a bang on the head.”

“I’m sorry to hear that. What do you need?”

“The hospital’s in bloody Telford so it’s a bit out of the way. Can you pop by our place after work and feed the dog, make sure he’s OK?”

“No problem. Why Telford?”

“She was doing some training over there.”

“Do you know what time you’ll be back?”

“No idea, late probably. Listen, thanks Gray.”

“No worries. Give Chris my best.”

“Will do.”

I hung up. In all of the panic I’d forgotten to ask him how his new job was going.

Christine was sitting up in bed with a bandage around her head when I arrived. She broke into a broad smile at the sight of me, quickly followed by a sudden rush of tears. I’d say that was the effect I’ve had on most women I’ve known. She leaned forward and opened her arms and we hugged tightly for a few moments.

After disengaging I looked at her closely, half-expecting to be able to see any signs of possible brain damage somehow manifesting on her face. Of course there was nothing, no visible sign of trauma in her features.

I loved that face, and now it was older than the one I initially fell for, and had the beginnings of crow's feet around the eyes and tiny bags beneath them, I loved it even more. My wife was the most beautiful person I'd ever seen, to me anyway. I loved the colour of her eyes, the green/grey of deep waters touched by sunlight. I loved her pert little button nose and her thin-lipped mouth, surrounded by an almond-shaped face. I could happily look at that face forever. I would be destroyed should I never be able to look upon it again.

The best thing about Christine's face was that I could see that love reflected back at me.

I reached for her again, hugging her tightly, tears forming in the corners of my own eyes.

"I'm sorry," she said.

"Don't be silly. Listen to me – those shoes are going in the bin, okay?"

"Not the bin, they're too good to throw away. I'll take them to the charity shop."

"Make sure you do. They're lethal"

"I should listen to you more often."

"Can I get that in writing?"

"Piss off."

I sat down on a slightly too small plastic chair by the side of her bed and held her hand. For the first time I noticed there were other beds in the ward and one or two other patients were looking at me. One smiled and nodded and I smiled back.

"How long before I can take you home?" I asked her.

"They haven't told me. I think I'm just waiting for test results. Will I be able to drive?"

"I doubt it."

"What about my car? It's still at the office."

"We can worry about that later. I can come back over with Graham tomorrow, maybe."

"OK." I could see her relax a little, as though the worry about what to do with the car had been taken away from her.

"What about Jack?" she asked, concern furrowing her brow again.

"Everything's fine, stop worrying. Graham's popped by the house to see to him."

"I don't want to be here overnight."

"Well, if you are we'll have to deal with it. Let's wait and see what the test results look like."

The test results were fine. The concussion was indeed mild and, apart from a sore head and a little bruising there would be no lasting effects. The doctor, a tall slim man who looked about fourteen, advised a good rest as a precaution with a couple of days at home doing nothing strenuous.

They said we could go just after half seven and I phoned Graham to update him whilst Christine got dressed. The drive home was quiet and uneventful, the heavy traffic of rush hour long since gone. It was starting to get dark as we turned the corner into our street and we were both suddenly alert as we saw the flashing blue lights outside our house.

"What the hell...?" I said.

We drove closer and saw that the ambulance was actually outside Mrs Tomlinson's. We parked up and got out of the car just as two paramedics brought a stretcher out. Whatever was on that stretcher – an inert lump just under five feet long – was completely covered by a blanket. A wisp of frizzy white hair was poking out of the top.

"What's happened?" I asked one of the paramedics, careful not to get in their way as they loaded the stretcher into the back of the ambulance.

"Heart attack," he said simply.

"Jesus. Is she... is she dead?"

"I'm afraid so. Do you know her?"

"I'm her neighbour."

"You might want to notify any next of kin," he said, climbing back out of the ambulance and closing the doors. His colleague walked around to the front of the vehicle and got inside.

"I don't think she had any. Do you know how it happened?"

"Hard to say. Probably had a shock of some sort."

Oh Jesus, no.

"Is there a dog inside her house?" I asked him, my throat dry.

"We didn't see a dog."

With that he too clambered into the front of the ambulance and, with the flashing lights suddenly extinguished, they slowly drove away. I walked back over to Christine, waiting by the garden gate.

"Is she dead?" she asked.

"Yeah."

"Poor old bag."

We heard a noise and saw Graham poking his head through the gap after partially opening our front door. He came out to join us.

"They've gone then?" he asked.

"Yes," said Christine.

"I heard this moaning sound about an hour ago, then there was this loud bang. I knew something was wrong."

"Did you call the paramedics?" asked Christine.

"Yeah. How is she?"

"She's dead." I said.

"Ooh. Dear."

I was feeling terribly, horribly guilty. I could just imagine what Mrs Tomlinson's last day on Earth had been like. Believing all my guff about swimming, she'd walked her dog – *Charlie* – to the quarry and had let it swim in the pool, where a monster had been waiting. She'd bore witness to her pet being pulled beneath the surface, violently snatched away and killed. She'd probably fallen to her knees, howling, maybe even entered the pool in an attempt to rescue her beloved pet.

The walk home must have lasted an eternity. Then, she'd have sat in her lounge, thinking about nothing else. The anguish must have torn her heart in two, and it had given up on her. And I'd done this. I'd killed her.

That pike wasn't the monster, I was.

"How are you, Chris?" asked Graham.

"A bit sore. Fine, compared to her."

"Come inside, both of you. I've got just the thing to cheer you up."

I followed my wife and brother up the path to the house.

"How come you're still here, anyway?" I asked him.

"You'll see."

As soon as we entered the house I could smell it. Graham had been cooking again. The most delicious aromas teased their way up my nostrils. Until that moment I hadn't realised just how hungry I was. My God, it smelled amazing.

"Sit yourselves down," he said, taking our coats and hanging them on the hooks in the hallway. We went through to the dining room. The table was already laid out. All around, the smell of delicate herbs and spices filled the air with warmth and joy – home cooking, done exceptionally well, is one of the most pleasurable things to experience. Graham was a magician with food.

"What is it?" I asked, sniffing the air.

"Wait and see."

He disappeared off into the kitchen and we heard the clatter of things being unloaded from the oven and trays being put onto racks.

"We should invite your brother over more often," said Christine. At that moment, sitting there smiling at me, her head wrapped in a neat bandage and her face slightly droopy with tiredness, I don't think she'd ever looked lovelier.

Graham walked in and placed a large roasting tin down onto the heat-proof mat at the centre of the table. Our meal was revealed. Scattered with herbs and resting in a thick sauce was a fish. A trout. Graham stood there with his hands on his hips, beaming at us. He couldn't have looked more pleased with himself.

I slowly lifted my head to look at him. Then, with my insides crawling and dread filling my veins with ice, I asked him a question.

"Gray - where did you get the fish?"

"What do you mean?"

"This fish, Gray, the fucking FISH! Where did you get it?"

I was hoping he'd say he picked it up on his way over but I already knew that he hadn't. I felt a sharp pain spreading along my left arm and my chest hurt like I'd been punched in the solar plexus. I felt breathless. The room span and I placed my hands on the table to steady myself.

"It was in the bath upstairs," he said. "What's up with him?" he asked Christine, nodding at me with a puzzled expression.

Everything seemed to catch up with me all at once and I keeled over, clutching my chest. Later, we would discover that it was nothing more than a panic attack but at the time I thought I was dying. At the time, curled up on the carpeted floor with my wife and brother reaching out for me, I wondered if this wasn't what I deserved and that somewhere in the room, invisible, two ghostly figures with perhaps half a dozen teeth between them were watching me suffer with grim smiles of satisfaction on their faces.

Other Books by Steve Roach

Short Story Collections

Resonance

The Hunt and Other Stories

Greatest Hits!

Novellas

Ruiner

People of the Sun

Conquistadors

Travel

Cycles, Tents and Two Young Gents

Mountains, Lochs and Lonely Spots

Step It Up!

Non-Fiction

Arcade Retro Classics

Illustrated Books For Children

Crackly Bones

The Terrorer

Amazon Reviews for Steve Roach's Stories:

I find that many books merge into one another in my mind and after a year or so I can't remember what it was about, or even what I found so special about it. With Steve Roach you know you'll never read another story like his. His work has a way of fixing itself in your mind forever. These stories are often not a comfortable read but if you want your ideas stretched and challenged, have a go.
Ignite, Amazon Review and Vine Voice.

This is a gem floating among the flotsam of self published stories on Amazon. The author grabs the attention of the reader early with a dark yarn told over a cold brew in worn down pub by the sea. What better place to hear a frightening tale of the black depths? Overtones of Poe can be felt throughout and the story didn't falter once as the horror continued to build.
Amazon.com review of The Whaler

I found the historical period to be accurately depicted, the gloomy coastal and shipboard settings to all ring true, and the central characters to have some genuine depth. With convincing scenery put quickly and efficiently in place and competent actors on the stage, the author proceeded to roll out a period American horror tale that kept me awake later than I had originally intended. I found myself needing to read just one more page until the entire story was satisfyingly done. That, in my opinion, is the sign of a well-made tale.
Amazon.com review of The Whaler

It's a well told tale and the descriptions of the hardships of life aboard a whaling ship, especially during the butchering, flensing and rendering stages are graphic and believable. I live near a town with a museum largely dedicated to the old whaling fleets and I've seen some of the tools used. Steve Roach knows of what he speaks.
Amazon UK review of The Whaler

I quite enjoyed this short story and despite it's bleak content felt it was well written and thought provoking. The blurb hinted at the dark turn the story takes yet I was still shocked by the finale. I felt there were various layers of hidden narratives; the cruelty of children, loyalty of a beloved pet and almost a Karmic climax.

Amazon UK review of A Dog's Life

I enjoyed this, it was a nice little read on a warm evening and I can honestly say I loved it, well written, poignant and engrossing, I just wish it had been longer, if I hadn't read it one sitting it would have been one of those books I would have laid awake at night thinking about and read some more as soon as I woke up next morning.

Amazon UK review of A Dog's Life

This is, without a doubt, the darkest and most disturbing book I've ever read....and I've read many. I will spend the rest of my life trying to forget it and wishing I'd never purchased it. I worry about the author.

Amazon.com review of A Dog's Life

The growing relationship between the man and the spider is a delight as we watch it unfold. Steve Roach has a dark side to his humour though. Things go downhill! This is a short story but as there's a small cast there is time for character development and the plot has a slight inevitability although I didn't see the final page coming. The author's writing style is skilful and accessible without being in any way simple. Short but sweet, this one, and well worth a read.

Amazon UK review of The Farda

If you have arachnophobia, then this story will probably make you very wary of reaching into a pile of bananas and keep you scanning the uppermost corners of your house. I really liked the connection and parallels between human and spider. It is also an example of how humans are more likely to act upon base instinct than they are aware of and how we imagine ourselves to be superior to all live forms. I enjoyed the read.

Amazon UK review of The Farda

Describing the ugliness that can happen in life is a delicate business, something that is handled sensitively in this unusual tale. It draws you in in a menacing way, and within its obvious desire to shock it also carefully balances a very human story throughout. Raw and thought provoking, I found it to be well written and an enjoyable read, which surprised me given the nature of its subject matter.
Amazon UK review for Bébé

This is a dark tale about a child born from a sexual assault that handles the subject in an honest manner. As a previous reviewer quite rightly said it is raw and thought provoking in a way that is both careful & sensitive. That being said, this book is not really for the faint-hearted or sensitive reader.
Amazon UK review for Bébé

This can't be called an enjoyable book; it's horrifying and fascinating though. Steve Roach often pushes at the boundaries of destructive relationships. It makes for the sort of book from which you can't look away - like a road accident. As I said, it's wrong to say it's enjoyable, showing as it does, scenes of abuse. It's a hard book to put down though!
Amazon UK review for Bébé

This, although ostensibly a story about fraternal hatred (it's much more than simple sibling rivalry!) seems rather deeper than its surface story. Twins who fought even in the womb and who spent their childhood fighting to the extent they were regulars at A&E finally seem to settle to ignoring one another. However, a love feud results directly in the death of one and indirectly the death of the other. We have all heard the term, 'Death is not the end,' and that's so true here. The depth of their mutual hatred is such that they still try to find ways to annihilate each other. The story, through some interesting descriptive prose, takes us much further, deeper, than you would imagine. Can hatred ever die? They say love never dies and hatred is just the other side of the coin. This is another intriguing idea from a man who can really come up with a good story line. The writing style is clear and unfussy but Steve Roach can use language well and pull the reader into a darned good tale.
Amazon UK review for Twins

This very short book made me laugh. Oh it shouldn't have but it did. Maybe I'm demented or I've been reading too many horror stories. This is a sick way to look at Santa. I took a star off because it's Christmas and I felt guilty.
Amazon UK review for XXXMAS (contains Glitter)

Another corker from Steve Roach. Amazing, thought provoking, scary stuff. Timeless – tackles our basic human insecurities.
Amazon UK Review for All That Will Be Lost

Printed by Amazon Italia Logistica S.r.l.
Torrazza Piemonte (TO), Italy

41982383R00105